Love is a Spi

G000167264

By Queen Irena

Published by
Chipmunkapublishing
PO Box 6872
Brentwood
Essex Cm13 1ZT
United Kingdom

Copyright © 2003 Chipmunkapublishing

A record of this book is in the British Library
ISBN 1 904697 00 3

Printed and bound
In Great Britain

THANK YOU MOTHER

Thank you,
For your love,
Dear Mother,
Thank you for your love.

For the kisses and caress,
And your night-time blesses,
Thank you for your love.

For the times you held me tight,
And our inspiring spiritual flights,
Thank you for your love.
Dear Mother,
Thank you.

For all the encouragement that you gave to me,
Showing me that I will always be,
A fruit from your sweet cherry tree,
Thank you.

When I think of you,
I begin to repair,
From my broken heart,
So I no longer despair,

Because with the foundation of your love within me,
I am no longer blind, now I can see.

Even the nights when he hurt you,
I always knew you,
You would never hurt me too.
So I thank you for your love,

My Queen Mother,
Jah bless you.

 I will always love you too

Sealed by Selah

ACKNOWLEDGEMENTS

I would like to firstly acknowledge and give thanks to Jah Rastafari because the I is I n I Most High.

Secondly, my children, I give thanks for my children. Through all their pains, they remained as true to me as their emotions would allow. They accepted my power (and lack of it) over them. They hold the truest of acknowledgement of me. Bless.

To Jason Pegler. I thank him for the opportunity to express my words in the way that is truly my own. He has given me hope for so many more that crave for a publisher that want lifesavers to come forward with their works.

LOVE IS A SPIDERS WEB
Emails to a Queen

FOREWORD

Edited by: Imani.

Livity Development Foundation (LDF)

In the language of Rastafarians, 'Queen' means the wife, the female partner of a man, her husband, 'King'. King and Queen should rule wisely and jointly to create and maintain a positive, loving and empowering environment for their children, brethren and sistren and the wider community.

Love is a Spider's Web details Shirley's transition from put upon wife raising seven children (two of whom are autistic) struggling to maintain her sanity while being in a loveless marriage. The story takes on her personal development after dealing with her abusive husband, who she puts out due to the negative effect on their children and her health. During the eight months approaching her fortieth birthday, Shirley becomes increasingly aware of her right to crown and call herself Queen and to take on her royal persona from an Afrikan perspective.

A new relationship inspires Queen Irena to come into being, and spurs her to reconnect with her aspirations of a better life and right to expect high quality love. She shares her wisdom by encouraging her readers to look within themselves, and to question statements and emotions, that hinder the recognition of ones spiritual self. The various descriptions of love and emotions that being a mother, lover, worker, and provider entails for Queen Irena are revealed within her written thoughts; erotic dreams, phrases, poems and prayers that challenge the role of Rasta women.

Women, who have loved but are oppressed by the destructive elements of their partners and question their own personal worth, will become aware of certain parallels in this story. Men who claim to be good friends, partners, lovers and fathers should also read this story, to gain insight into how they are perceived by the outside world.

Love is a spider's web provides a refreshing view of how the complexities of life affect one black woman who happens to be a mother and a Rasta woman. She spontaneously communicates her experiences via email to her special Queen (Imani), as the fastest way to record her responses and to pass on truth and knowledge. Queen Irena will help you to speak your truth clearly and to enjoy doing it.

This is a truly touching and beautiful display of companionship, respect, friendship, pain, forgiveness and desire through royalty. You recognise your true wealth as a result of reading this story.

I PRAY FOR YOU

OPENING

As I walk in this love,
I pray for you.
As I breathe in this love,
I pray too.

Love and prayer,
Are two of the same,
So I pray for you,
And others too,
In this I have no shame.

Yes at times I am the riddler,
This much I know.
There is no other way,
To explain how I have grown,
Besides the natural flow.

Of what has been written,
And of what has to be,
A most powerful friendship,
Between the I within you
And the I within me.

Prayers are not always recited,
As words cannot at times,
Connect us with the above,
But the Livity that we find ourselves in,
Even at times when we think,

There is no love, we have.

Your life is full, this much is true,
But if you had all you desired,
Looked at what was behind it,
You might never know,
That your dreams had come true.

Strange as it may sound,
You are still blessed.
With every waking pain,
So that when you release,
You will continue to be praised.

For the heights of the journey,
That you will reach,
When the time is right for your flight,
My God, can you cope,
With that kind of delight.

You're right to hold back,
At times when you do,
Because it shows,
That you already know,
The Most High will never forget nor leave you.

Even if you say you,
Do not believe or are pissed with him,
You still go back and retrieve,
Him from your spiritual bin.

Your royalty joins us,
And you pray again because,

Of your hopes and your dreams.
Just in case you were wrong,
About your fate so you find,
Your faith and move up in your belief

INTRODUCTION

The fundamental inspirations that have aided the birth of this book have been from the lessons I have learned throughout the writing of it. They are the lessons of love and the impact they have made on the relationships that I have with those I love, and of those that are in my love and my life. I must say I am loved in the deepest of ways that contain a place that I may fly to, when ever I am in need. I give the most thanks to the highest power, as I feel him inside me when I am both glad and sad. He lifts me and saves me and cleanses my soul and I am filled with gold. Now, I just cannot keep that to myself, can I?.

I have tested a few of my chapters on a sample of members within the community and I have since become

more aware, of the enormous issues that are being faced by those around me, not just by women. I have also become positively in tuned with deep feelings that men hold in relation to their own lessons of love, man, its deep. "How did you come up with the title?" I am asked. Well, all the webs that I had seen never seemed to have a fly caught in the middle, except if there is evidence of one being captured elsewhere and dragged to the middle to be devoured. The web appears to be strong, yet it is so delicate. Wonderfully defined paths, but equally beautiful are the diversions between them. The temptations are many and tug at us as we become stuck within relationships whether it be intimate or otherwise. Sometimes we become stuck in situations that are so sweet but can only lead to heart ache, yet still we hold on for dear life. Are we waiting for the Most High spider to come and play with us or to devour us? Maybe someone with nothing to do would come along and destroy the web as they walk past, not knowing that we ever existed. Maybe we await the almighty spider to just hold and carry us back to our central being where he resides for us to witness and take note of the power that we all hold within our souls. Why do so many fear spiders so? Tiny ones are feared too. (Yes, and their empty webs).

University taught me a few lesson though. The hardest one was the one that demanded me to meet the dead lines for those essays. So many bloody essays "They're taking the piss." I would be up laughing with the sun many a morning even after managing a spot of passion for the oppressor. So glad I can fake it, and that I could meet the deadlines. I think there may be a joke there

somewhere, but got too much to say. With me, well, University taught me to never include (I) in my writings, and to reference and counter reference. Well I reclaim I self that I have brought back to I surface. Hell, I can even go deeper and reveal to you the I within the I am in I n I. There, that's more like it, I give thank Jah Rastafari.

I have had fun while writing this book too, as when I say, "Love is a spider's web", my respondents begin to describe a web and talk of various issues they happen to be facing at that moment. Yes, it is all about love, so they begin to depict the various feelings that using a web as an example had brought up for them.

Even more than that, were the times spent putting this book together. On occasions I would look up, and notice the sun had arisen and was laughing at me still typing. This would not stop me though, as each time I wrote, it was spontaneously completed before I could sleep, as my writings were from my thoughts at that time. I could never take notes or record what I wanted to write, as it did not feel real or help my words to flow onto the paper and bring my story to life. My youngest son was over active with his autism and did not sleep during the day, and wouldn't sleep before 11pm each night. He would sometimes put me to sleep himself, and I would not awake until just before up time and you know what that's like (No, I can only address that one to the Queens).

There are lesson to learn and actions to be taken that may seem unfair, harsh or even beyond your sweetest of dreams at times, but lessons none the less. Having said this, over standing it all can also be a burden, like the dark cloud that seems to follow one at times, but give thanks for the over standings all the same.

Bearing this in mind, I am very much aware that I cannot stand and say how the web of the spider has affected the kings out there; they would have to give account for themselves. My experiences merely express the effect that those in my life have had on me, and of whom I love. I do however work and love hard to bring support and joy to those within my soul, so I may receive from them the love and care that I too need in return.

I therefore dedicate and introduce a definition of a spider's web, by a man that knows it. I also pray that it may empower more over standing towards the plight of the real man.

Written by Shaun McRae
22nd June 2002

Love is a confusing
Situation but it is also
A powerful emotion
Love is a tease and
A temptation
You can't over stand
Love
You just have to go
With the flow
Love is a spider waiting
To consume us

Love is a blessing
Love is a curse love
is a light in our darkest
Hour
Love is a test love is
A prize love is a web
That catches us all
Love is a spider waiting
For it's pray
Love is a spiders web

Love makes us laugh
Love makes us cry
Love weave's a web
That controls us all
Don't try to find it
It will find you
Love can also be
A threat too love
Is a spider's web
That consumes us all

Love is an inspiration
Love is life love is
Destruction love is
Belief
Love is destitution
How do we make it
Work
Love is a game that's
Played if we know all
The rules
Love is a spider's web

© 2002 S. McRae

15

1.LOVE IS A SPIDER'S WEB
Emails to a Queen
Insight to The Woman

Throughout my endeavours to maintain a positive Livity, I have continually trod along my road, picking up the broken pieces (my children) from an oppressive marriage. I call them the broken pieces at this time, as they are. Broken, because family life for them had not turned out to be as smooth as they had excitedly hoped. Well, the only comparisons being of what they witness on the television. I am not saying that they watch a lot, as I always seem to intervene when I notice the children on the screen are running the show.

They (my children), are quite contented with the fact that parents are subordinate to their children, they always seem to be apologising for the discipline they had chosen against what (I believe), to be total disrespect being displayed by the children in the programmes. It appears to give some kind of release for my royal family, from the lack of love between their own parents, along with the rules and regulations that I place on them, so they may see the truth behind all the lies. Their lives are tough, so I aid them with outside professional support, as well as my own professionalism joined with my true and pure love maintained by the royal guidance that I receive. Jah be with them.

Apart from the fact that it is seven children (the eldest two became my children by marriage, two of my birth children happen to be Autistic) that I mother, merely adds to the enormity of my workload. It also gives some kind of indication that I could not possibly have had time to work, study for two diplomas, a degree, care for a brother with mental illness, chair a management committee for a local youth club, go to the gym and to the local pool, attend every parents evening, and counselling session, take part in empowerment programmes that aid the implementation of good inclusion policies within the community, meditate, plait hair, make time to share with my Queens and Kings, organise cultural events and write my autobiography. I am living proof that it has been done. That is not to say that there are not others that had done the same, far from it. We are everywhere.

For a start, I have not mentioned all the other tasks that behold a woman, neither have I thrown in the never ending lessons learnt along the way from the clothes worn, looks, the sexual innuendos, games, shames, lies, disrespect, judgemental, loving and nursing burdens that we carry.

Of course on top of it all, there are the red days that we all face at regular intervals. Do we stop for this? No, even the adverts make us out to be fakes, as our protection become
wafer-like and light as a feather, hell they even have wings. No medical evidence that show the flood normal women have, or intermittent gushes that happen at times because of the extreme stresses we face. The adverts simply imply that we go about our daily chores with empty heads. Nothing for those that have no choice but to keep going while they pad themselves up, preventing the remnants of the babies they lose along the way from showing. Yes, this book will hit you like a ton of bricks occasionally. Sister, you can cry, it's all right, I know the

pain. I will love you forever for feeling the way I do, because you truly know babes. Brother, what can I say? I love you too, but boy, have I got news for you. No I won't mention bills or money right now, as that is a whole new book and it would not be as light as this one.

These are serious times for serious people that happen to live in reality. We all have our stories to tell. We all need to have one to listen to us, and to hold us so tight; we could sleep forever from the effect of that one embrace. (Yes, without your hands wondering about us, just this once or maybe even twice, dare I say for longer)? It is so important to us that we would give the whole world, and pay dearly for it. But wait a minute; did I not get that a whole lot once in my lifetime? I must have. Yes mummy; I do remember those times, I miss them so. I miss you too, my mummy. "Oh god, help me to not need her so. Jah please help me to be strong like she was and still is. She is always on my mind".

I have said many a time "One day I am going to write a book about my life" I have usually said it in response to an event that had led me to question how on earth I would cope. I just pick myself up and get on with it. Admittedly, I have driven myself to the extent of disability (Yes five years ago I walked with a stick to aid me). I have had moments of despair, and had left everything and had walked out, leaving my husband with the children without notice. That was not difficult, as I had never left with the intention of never coming back; it certainly did not equal the time he had spent away from us all. No, his time could never be accounted for not by him. I just nursed myself and (regrettably him) through the diseases that admitted he had time away. I had taken the odd day or two out of the everyday, as a protest against the lack of love and respect shown to me by my husband that had filtered into the behaviour of the children towards me. There were times when I had become suicidal because of the sentence I had been under, as there just did not seem to be time left for me to recognise myself. I began to set my clock just in case I fell asleep while waiting for the youngest to asleep.

It had become important for me to identify a time for me, even if that meant staying up to watch a film at 2.30am. At least I had time all to myself (Yes I still do it now and then, just like you). The only thing is, there were times when I made myself go to bed so he would not think I was staying up for him. I paid for staying up the next day when I did with him, as school always started the same time each day and did not make allowances for overworked and oppressed mothers who sacrificed their bodies as a means to have peace at odd hours.

I am grateful for the calm after the storm of the morning rush hours, at least though as sometimes I feel like I am floating on air with the sounds and thoughts of the blessed children singing so brightly, in assemblies all over the world. Their voices are so powerful to hear, you just cannot help but say 'ah'. So, just before I start feeling the guilt about the rushing and the tempers reached before the departing, I give thanks for them and pray for their souls (and their educators), until my children return back to me their head Queen.
Queen Irena
LOVE IS A SPIDERS WEB
                    Emails to a Queen

2. OPENING THE ASPECTS OF MY SOUL

Baring ones' soul in order to show oneself can be risky. I say this because I have a slight fear of what reactions my readers' may have when they read. "Why?" you might ask. Well, that is part of what this book is about. It is also about my aspirations, desires, needs, hurt and pain as well as gains. This book is aimed at the adult reader, lay and professionals alike that care to be inspired by the expressions of a love like no other. You know who you are. You need to rise and fly but there is too much for you to do beforehand. You cannot be seen reading, as it would simply imply that you have nothing else to do. What will be your response when you do read, and are enlightened by my emotions? Will you be able to cope or even to over stand the heights that you are about to travel to?

There are those that wish to know the truth behind me. Hell, I wish to over stand to the fullness, the truth behind me. That is not to say that I must therefore divulge my inner most emotions, no. I have a story that I wish to tell and that you wish to read about, so this is not only for me, it is also for those of you that yearn to make this journey with me. The transitions that I make and the emotions I experience, will inspire you to the point where you will tap into your place, where you need to go. It is the true one within you that we all have. It will awaken you into action through me. Having expressed this, I feel that I may also go on to say, that the reactions I have to my experiences belong to me, so your personal reactions to these emotions therefore belong to you. If what you read of me happens to awaken you into positive actions, I give thanks. The thoughts of seeing others releasing their royal powers and glowing about the place would certainly increase the glow within me.

Who am I? Well I am the, 'I am' that dwells within the I in me. I be, I see, I feel, I create, and I move with the Most High inside me, around me, over me, in front and behind me. I am therefore also the Most High. 'I'.

No, don't turn away from me, look at me. Do you overs what the I has just expressed to you? Why do you hesitate? Is this too real for you? Or is it that you can no longer confer with me. Well, don't stop looking at me, or loving me, wanting or needing me, because this I is also a Queen that was placed on this earth to carry out missions and confessions of the lessons of love through my transitions that I will now share with the world. "Love is a spider's web" captures the emotions that you have within you too, because I hold the most desires, like you do. There is also within me a power that will take your breath away and aid you in your flight too, so I would urge you to be true to your own energies while remaining true to the energies that this I, will give to you. This I is Queen Irena.

The Most High gave me a gift last night. I received it with the most thanks, as I needed to liberate the passions that I held within me. I prayed for guidance, peace and love, and waited. It was a long wait. I almost fell asleep, but was aware of his warm sensation inside my head. I could not get up due to the pressure on my body. He had come. At last he had come. Warm air came too, and it blew onto me. I opened my clothes and closed my eyes. My breasts were firm and my nipples hard. The slightest

21

touch of them made me breathless. I panted. (I could never turn him away or object, as This Must Be).

I rubbed both nipples with the palms of my hands, and I was so very hot. I had my dance partner and I wanted him so. I knew it was he, but I could not open my eyes to visually witness him take me. I felt him and, oh God, I cannot describe this being with me. I became tense and was afraid, but he whispered his words to me and I instantly responded. "Please take me," I begged. I wanted to feel him, and then he was there. This was what I desired and what I had prayed for and I received him with the greatest of pleasure.

My releases were very intense, and it was hard to breath. My mouth filled with fluid and my womb ached, but that was only part of it. I jerked after this as I had spurts of continued orgasms that I could not control. I felt every part of my soul engulfed by this intense pleasure, and I was touched again very gently. My skin was so sensitive to his touches that it made me cry with the sweetness of it all. I was kissed all over. I could hardly cope with it, as the feeling was so high and so sweet. It happened again, but this time it was difficult to cry out, as the feeling was extremely powerful, I could only whimper until it was over, and he had left.

These times are most real for me, as I have vivid memories of a great and safe power deep within my soul, where I continually want it to be. I had always known it to be from a most high power. This is not to say that I have no need for all this with a one that has simple earthly needs, as I most certainly do. I see those with their desired companions and I feel pain, deep pain over the loss and rejection by those that had tried to love me, but could not. As I said before, I was placed on this earth on a mission to give my ultimate love and to be with a one that I can receive the same from. I have found the journey to be most threatening and totally unsafe for me at times.

I say this because of the burdens that I witness my love had placed on those whom I love. It is really not easy for me as I am sent to them at a time when they are not ready to or are unable to receive me. This is when the gift of passion comes to me through the Most High order so that I may continue to release and fly (for the moment) from the pain that I often feel. This pain is deep, and has been with me for longer then I can even remember.

I have always had a need to release passion, so had spent many sweet moments being aided with this privately in my bed as a young girl. I thought it was a natural experience that we all had (I did not dare ask anyone though). I was always able to experience pleasure, and had orgasms. No, I was not taught or shown. It is so easy to set alarm bells off within ones head here; I know those kinds of thoughts. No, (I talk of my personal pleasurable releases that were safe and not invoked by an abuser) these pleasurable moments, made me became orgasmic most nights. Having said this however, I have not up to this day, found one that could give to me, the complete passion that I had always needed, and desired, but had been able to give to myself, or to receive alone. That hurts me a whole lot as I have given everything that I want back, but my empty space is never filled. This is so painful that it swells my heart and my whole being, even while I write about this emotion. I have had no choice but to call on the Most High, who gives to me all that I desire.

I do however, have more of what I desire now then I have had before though. A new
Aspect of my soul is being continually filled by the love from another being that I can feel inside me, whether he is physically with me, or at other times. This being and I have a bond that can only be matched with what I have with that of the Most High, so do not be surprised, as it is true. During this stage in my life, the most high has enabled him to see and know the being within me that I had hidden from the rest of the world. The love and inspiration that he has given to me, is felt deep within my soul and has guided me through my most sacred of emotions. I must say here, that what had been released by the I within me had come out of the ultimate love that I feel for him, and how I have responded to the effects of these emotions. I cannot say that it has been a smooth journey for me, far from it. In fact, it has been the hardest journey of my life and my love, and I mean that most sincerely.

The aspects of my soul that had been and are still being tested are like a never-ending road. I have been tested to the very depths of my being by this love and need that I contain. I have felt every emotion possible, and have at times cried like a baby over it all. It is as extreme as my special orgasms. At times, I have felt that the love I hold would bring about the death of the I within me. Yes, I know I have your utmost attention now.

It is also amazing to me at times, how much I have been able to bear. I have awoken and happened to dread the prospects of yet another new day without the complete love that I desire, but the day ends soon and before it ends, I had forgotten about the pain that I feel. I remember that my Most High god is there for me. He is my food, and I am filled. I sometimes feel that time is running out for another to fly with me, as I see no signs regarding the prospect of another that is both willing and able to experience such ultimate pleasures. I see no signs of a one that can fill me in the same way that I am able to fill those in my love. It is not that there is none capable of meeting my needs; I just see fear in their eyes at times when they look at me. This is even from the special Kings in my life.

It certainly aids my feelings of disappoint and hurt at the fact that I have not experienced a King beside me that is strong enough to admit he desires my ultimate loving touches and to be true to me, as I would admit I desire his and be true to him. I wonder if I have frightened them away with my status or physical approach or spiritual presence through my reasonings. I wonder if my love is too much for them to experience. I wonder if it is too much for you. Only time with the I am within me can possibly aid in the journey through the I am within you.

Queen.

3.LOVE IS A SPIDER'S WEB
Emails to a Queen
Fulfilling The Need

My Dear Sweet Queen.

Jah has been with me more than ever now. Having said this, I still feel a need to be fulfilled within my soul. I feel that I have held so much pain and sadness through the years that I have forgotten what it is like to let go. I suppose I have let go in the past, it's just that I have not until now recognised to the full that I have always been a Queen (or should I say walking the path of a princess), Why is it so hard for us to see the royalty within us, I wonder?

I needed some royal attention that would help with my need to release some royal passion that I held within me. I decided to take the plunge, and make a call. Success. He was ready. What a release, but of course not enough to satisfy my soul. Oh, he treated me good, real good and I had a very exciting romp but (you know what I mean), it kept me smiling for a great start to the New Year. I felt like a naughty little schoolgirl that just had a very tasty lunch that no one has tasted except me. There was still of course deep within me, desires in other areas. It felt so deep. He kept appearing within me and I saw his name everywhere.

All I could think of was my sweet love (KING). I have spent a lot of time with my King, who shows me love in such a sweet way that it mystifies my very being. Sometimes I feel extremely passionate towards him and some times I feel my soul is taken over when I think of him, or when I am with him. Why am I so drawn to him?

26

It is not just a sensual pull with me, it is happening to him also and we both know it.

He has given me the love and care that I truly need, he has seen me at my home, and I have been with him at his place. Jah knows how great his power is. Our families have been engulfed together. His mother (who is also a Queen) has taken to my family and my children, who love her too. They adore my King, and it has happened so naturally that there is no pressure for us to be together. I feel this Love in such a beautiful way, that this family had become a total support network for all the children and myself. His family had provided me with the much needed emotional healing and physical care where possible.

The children's father (Omar), well I wish him all good, but since he has realised that we will no longer return together, he is having difficulty coping with it. He wailed like a baby during a conversation I had with him recently. He now says he no longer wishes to see the children. Yes, he leaves it to me to explain, and of course we (Women) sometimes lie and tell them things like "Daddy is not very well at the moment, and the doctor said he needs to rest so that when he feel better he will have great energy to spend time with his children. He says he loves you so much" (Maybe I shouldn't have told him that I had passion with another), but I am at least glad I was able to be honest with him about the children's needs and their love of him as they would be totally destroyed if I talked to them like he did.

My (King) had supported my actions towards him and showed me that my self worth was lowered each time I reflected on the oppressive experiences faced with my children's father. King had become open to me in a way that aided me in the acknowledgement of the I within me, therefore he protected my personal, emotional and spiritual being. Total respect (High quality love) most certainly applied right here between and within us. It could only be called royal to me.

I have a Queen in my life that is tapping into her royalty. She too had moved on from her own oppressive marriage become open and was within royalty with another (What a buzz. With this being so, her former husband visits me. (Why me?) Its not that I don't like him, he is able to help the boys keep their computer in order and they like that. I make sure he has something to eat and is compensated for his time, but he tries to draw me into his sadness of the break up and expects me to aid him in his attempts to reconciliate his ended relationship.

We never spent a moment in any personal conversation before, in fact not even about other things either. The man never gave me the time of day and now he is here all the time; wants me to comfort him and wishes to sit with me in my bedroom. He spends a lot of time round the computer (Of course) I am beginning to feel uneasy with it. I know he is lonely and all that, but boy, my vibes will never go there. So he fixes the children's computers, and I keep out of the way and tell him when to go when I am ready. He has just walked into my room as I type this e-mail so I will sign off until the next episode.

Jah

Queen Irena

4.LOVE IS A SPIDER'S WEB

Emails to a Queen
Standing Firm

Sweet Queen Imani

I pray that all is well with you and your royal family.

As for I sis well all is well. I have been able to express myself safely with those (including yourself) that love and care for me.

Tsion is managing well but still at times has pains, which I am a little concerned about, as I know what that kind of pain can progress to. Although I had had many pregnancies, Tsion's pregnancy is a strange one as she had become near to death with the amount of vomiting she was doing. Worst or all was the fact that she had never been in a relationship (you know) she certainly did not go to parties or had fun with her friends visiting her. Neither did she chat excitedly about fun that happened. Yes, she was the original 'Home Girl'. She also however had deep pain within her that needed a great deal of nursing so it could be released (Like we all have). Anyway, I am keeping an eye on the vibes for her safety.

I must say, I do look forward to the time I spend with sweet King as he listens to me and aids in the healing process for me and I do feel that the same goes for him, he also says that this is so. Thank God there is a one that I may share with and to see the purity within.

I have had a few days peace from Omar's calls. I must say it is interesting that he is feeling some of what I felt when he disrespected and deceived me during our time together. (Not that I have now put that on him in any way). He knows now that it is not possible for him to do that anymore, as he knows that Jah is with me, that is why he wants a piece of me so that he can move on, but girl, he did not do that with me so he will have to do that without me. I have moved on and my royal stance will not bow down or sell myself out.

I sometimes think that maybe one day I will awaken and find that all that went on between us was a dream, but no, it was nightmare. The babies I had lost, the tears and the years spent praying for just one live child to love until I die. I remember that Jah had given me my children to love in the best way possible so returning to Omar would surely mean death for me therefore only death for my gifts. 'Not on your Nelly'. I would live forever if the alternative would be to leave them to grow with him. Strong words I know, but with my very being this must be so Imani.

So Queen I do hope that your Prince enjoyed his trip out on Saturday. He was worn out when we got back. Give him and his brother a kiss for me I know you are glad they are back at school (we all feel the same) its not that we want to get rid of them, its just that its the teachers turn now (Jah bless every empowering effort that they put in to the care of our fruits).

Signing off now

Queen.

5.LOVE IS A SPIDER'S WEB

Emails to a Queen
Confirming The Web

Greetings Queen

I am sorry that I couldn't respond to your call last night, or was it this morning.

Yes I was with King. We had just finished talking about the Queens in my life. We talked of you also. We just began to talk about us and the phone rang. It only rang once before I picked it up and it went off. Now that is strange.

Anyway, King told me of his love for his Queen and that he knows from the very bottom of his soul that she is what he wants, but he also said that I had brought out the very same feelings from him towards me and that his heart is being torn in two. He held me and kissed me with love and complete passion and I kissed him in the very same way. My whole being felt, what it was supposed to feel, but with reservations. All I wanted for myself was his love at that moment but we both held onto each other's hands tightly in silence and wanted one another but we could not continue. We both felt it and Queen it was so powerful, but I don't know what happened to either of us then I just remember that I could hardly breathe.

While I was getting ready to go to his place last night, my old friend made new on New Years Eve called. When I saw his name come on the mobile I nearly dropped, but he just called to say that he has not forgotten me and will call me again. I was so glad that he was not asking me to be with him last night, because nothing was going to keep me away from this intense love that I felt within me. The energy between King and I is so high that it can be frightening at times but not in a bad way, in a way that I am not able to describe at this present time. He said he wanted to make love to me and that he knows that I love him as he sees it in my eyes (girl, I thought about my eye liner). You must be hanging onto the computer right now. I had to write to you about this, as all I can think of is King right now. He seems to have been placed within my soul but we can only take things a day at a time. Jah only knows what this is all about and what will happen to this love. It may read strange but I know this is big, I can feel it in my bones.

We both seemed to be in a spin but managed to agree that it was not a good idea to move more intimately right then, so we peeled our hands apart from one another and I left with a limping heart, and could barely breathe. I must have looked back at him a thousand times as I walked down the stairs and through the front door as he followed my movements. This was overwhelming, as my heart was on fire just like I know his was too. Is this what I felt it was only not what I was taught? Love I mean. Well, this love has me stuck while I float on air. This is a Web.

Tune into the next "Love is a Spiders Web"

Queen Irena

6.LOVE IS A SPIDER'S WEB
Emails to a Queen
Encounter V Responsibility

Greetings Queen.

My life has been quite eventful; It's just knowing where to start at times. Here goes.

Over the weekend I was busy what with Tsion still in the hospital. She seems to be having an emotional at the moment that she will take time to express. It must be hard for her to adjust to a new life when she has hardly understood the last one. I pray that she will find love in the joy of expressing it to a one so pure as a baby. I know this will properly cut short the time that she needs to spend with her friends and herself, but she can still have that if she works hard for it. I must say that she has been so supportive of me and her brothers', one cannot wish for a more caring daughter, I only pray that she will go on to experience the love and care that she will need in her new life as a mother and as a woman. She expressed to me that she feels she has let me, but even more herself down for thinking that this man loved her and that she fell for it (Don't we all at times in our lives), hard I know but I wore that T shirt, apparently still too.

I have spent quality time with my sweet King, which filled me to the brim. On Monday this week we had an encounter that we were not prepared for, so it did not go well. It also opened us up in a way that is a little frightening. I suppose you are asking me what happened. Well it was so emotional for us both that it left a bitter taste, but that is not to say that I wish it did not happen, its just that the feelings I have had about making love with the man was highly charged and also very explosive within the both of us. I must say I was suddenly afraid that this was not the right time for us and that instead, we just needed to caress each other in order to have peace at that time. I know this is so true for many, but somehow, we allow lust or extreme want take control in place of what we really need. We all need a love to call our own and to hold and comfort and cherish us so deeply. I know for me with the complete desire and purity that I felt for King, I assumed that maybe he was ready for me, as I was for him. Man was I wrong, seems I'm not the only one with baggage to carry.

I needed him so badly today you know, so much so that, I had to roll on my bed and ask Jah for mercy. Yes, you better believe it. I have never ever had to do that for anyone before. I cried and asked Jah why I have to feel this way; of course it made no difference. All I could do was to give in to this feeling. My body was taken over by a most powerful being for something that I had no control over. I sent King a text calling him to me showing him that I needed him to be with me now, girl I know he had to go to work, so we were both strong and held ourselves. I did finally call his mobile and talked with him. He seemed very low. Guilt was upon me but my sexuality was strongly upon me too as his was it seemed.

As for you know whom; well I had to tell him to keep his hands off Tsion, as she was my responsibility now. He had the nerve to go to the hospital and upset her, telling her, she was responsible for the end of his marriage to me. I am so glad she is old and wise enough to know that she is no more responsible for our break up then are any of the children. I have made it clear to all the children that, throughout the ups and downs between myself and their father, I have had the utmost respect for them and will cherish the joy and happiness shown both towards each other and to myself while maintaining themselves as children with a right to true love and complete care from their parents. There will never be blame placed upon any of my children from me regarding any problems faced between their father and myself.

Tsion may be out of the hospital this evening, as she is feeling a lot better now. I give thanks for that, Jah. I also give thanks for myself, as I would not have to be up and down so much. I just pray she quickly comes to terms with the pregnancy as her gloomy face and vibes will make her baby uneasy which could eventually make it more difficult for us all.

Tune in to the next episode of "Love is a Spiders Web"

Queen Irena

7.LOVE IS A SPIDER'S WEB
Emails to a Queen
Perceptions Of Love

Greetings Queen

It has been hard both to find time and to gather my thoughts and feelings on writing this book. My emotions are somewhat extreme, or should I say heavy and at times hard to deal with. Since Wednesday, as I told you, things have been a little stressful to say the least.

Firstly, Tsion came home on Wednesday. Mum (King's mum) brought her home in a cab. Tsion is finding it hard to get her head around everything, but no doubt I will help her to sort out all the problems as we women usually do, along with aiding the other children from the distress of witnessing their sister in a sick state. We will all work on the issues of her being pregnant, without them ever having evidence of a male figure that had been know as her companion let alone cared enough to visit or take her out. Arran punched the floor after learning of Tsion's pregnancy. This I know is because of the constant name calling that he had witnessed his father promote toward his sister. (He is not sure whether this meant that the names were true) He never saw her with a man and he at least knew, there was a friendly smile or even a kiss involved between a man and a woman before a pregnancy happened. (Being the observant sweet child that he is) Thank God the children have some over standing regarding the need to have love that they know had not been experienced by their sister. We totally under estimate our children's' perceptions of love.

As for King, well he is finding it very hard to be at peace with the plans he has made with his life and the support he needs to give to his mother. He is very low and is struggling to keep it together. I know part of it all is his feelings for me, but I can only be there when he needs me if I am available, which I really want as I feel great around him. He gives me so much. He has talked with his mum (while he cried bitterly about his feelings for me, and she says he must choose between me and the other woman he says he has loved for a long time. She is fed up of the love pains she has witnessed him face, and a little angry, while at the same time feeling the effect of the rejections she too is living with. Love truly is a spider's web. Make no mistake about it.

I am left feeling that King must choose her as I do not want him to regret being with me, I have been told this so many times by Omar. On the other hand, I feel it would be wonderful to just melt in King's arms and him in mine. Its not even just the physical want either, I actually would love for him and me to be an item, because I love him deeply, but (There is always a but) because that is what we are all made of is it not? Tsion also told me that when King and mum went to visit her in the hospital, he expressed his feelings towards me. He asked her if she would be upset if he had feeling's for me. She told me that she said it was because, if I were happy, the whole family would be. (You better believe it girl).

I am not really feeling too well today, feel a little low in spirits but as you know trod ding is something else, because no matter what is going on in ones intimate life, other influences will get the better of you. There is still a tiny voice within me (the almighty father), saying "Believe and I will be with you" Solace enough for me.

Love is a spider's web.
Queen.Irena

8. LOVE IS A SPIDER'S WEB

Greetings Queen

The Spider has taken hold of me and I am feeling a little despondent right now.

I feel that Tsion is beginning to understand that life pains and choices are hard to bear at times as she is now aware that a man can just pretend to love a woman when it suits him and leave, but also that this can leave many others in turmoil. As for Tsion, well she will have to take full responsibility for something that started with a decision that was made between her and another. At times it's just history repeating itself. Yet the next generation of my flock staring the same old cycle. When will it ever stop Jah? When.

It's so hard to even write about what else has happened, but you know I have to. Its King, everything has been a little too much for him so he had become very distraught, so was taken to the crisis centre by his cousin and brother. They wanted to section him, so I had his mother crying and heart broken on the phone, which started on the walk down the hill to work from 1pm until around 9pm.

When I got into work I saw that the result of an X ray done on Ezekiel which showed a bone disease. I had an appointment with him right after work to discuss it with the doctor, which was ok. Apparently it is to do with his growth spurt and growing pains, and all that. He still needs to see a specialist, but I was told that this situation would disappear once he passes fifteen. Unfortunately he will have to avoid contact sport and can only partake in swimming. Ezekiel needed a lot of reassurance, which I gave to him and always will. He is a great athlete and is particularly good at running, but it will only aggravate his condition and render him disabled, so he will have to wait. He will be fine, as he is good at over standing when it comes to reasoning with me, my sweet prince. In fact he is my first blessed fruit. Jah alone knows the truth my prince gives to me. It ripens the powers within me to be. Selah. When I see him sad I feel my sheer existence is destabilised. I try not for him to witness when I too am distressed as it most certainly disturbs his being. Warning enough for me.

Last night I went to King's yard. He chatted with me a little before I went in to see his mum. He said he felt a lot better as he managed to talk with the woman tenant (who he had a relationship with and ended it around a year ago) and they have come to a friendship agreement. I was glad. Her showing him that she now had a thing going with his stepbrother, was upsetting him. You are most likely thinking Lord God, is there no end to the Spiders Web? To answer that, I can only say "Not really".

I chatted with his mum, then I went to see him in his room and he seemed upset. He was sitting on his bed looking at the floor. He said, "I feel a little empty". I asked him if it was because of the end of the above relationship. He said, "That made living here bearable. When I leave here I would be much happier anyway". I asked him if he had anything he wanted to say to me he should not be afraid to, as I was open and was am not afraid. He told me "Everything is good between us". I told him that I would have a chance to have a day to myself next week and ask him if he would like to join me. He said, "Yes". I went back to chat with his mum and soon left. He brought me home.

He stood at the door and held me tight and left looking terrible, so I phoned him when he got back home. He said, "I didn't tell you something". I said "tell me now". He said, "I feel suicidal, but I won't do it". I asked him to come back to me now, to get a cab and that I would pay. He cried and said he had to go. Well girl, I sent him five txt begging him to come back. No response. After thirty minutes, I called his mobile, he answered. He was crying but said he was tired. I told him to just sleep and I would phone him in the morning.

Could I sleep? You must know the answer to that one. I phoned about 8.30. He was asleep but answered his phone, said he was ok and asked me to call him later. I told him I would phone before I left for work. When I called, there was no answer from his mobile. I phoned the landline and was told that both him and mum were not around. There was no response from my calling his mother's mobile either. I must admit I was so worried; I could barely manage to collect my thoughts. She called me later on my way to work. I could hardly control my upset over what had happened to this sweet King in my life. Why was I in such a state? Well I am not made of stone, but more than that, I truly love him. His mother however did not want me to go to him, which upset me even more. I suppose she was doing the right thing considering that she was aware that we both had deep rooted feelings flying around for each other and that this had most likely contributed to the crisis that King was going through.

I called at the house this morning, Mum answered the door. She looked so mashed. I was doing some cleaning when mum called me to say that King was upset that I was there. He had told his brother who told her. So she cried and said she was sorry. I told her that I would go. I left.

I am pleased that he was able to say what he did and I told mum and Ian that I know my being around may be very difficult for him so it was expected, but as you know, I must be feeling something. I know I will continue positively and I am still Queen Irena. I can of course also admit here that it hurts like it is meant to as while typing the tears have hindered me no end.

Tune in to the best of "Love is a Spider's Web"

Jah Jah

Queen.Irena

9. LOVE IS A SPIDER'S WEB
Emails to a Queen
Sensual Awakenings

Greetings Queen Imani

Jah has been around as usual. His divine power has carried me though as Love has its way with me.

Tsion is vomiting again so she may well be in hospital soon. She has a specialist appointment tomorrow that will advise her on what needs to be done. She is getting emotional support from the young women's resource centre, which I have sorted as it has been an organisation that I had been constantly connected with. This area Tsion had chosen not to take note of until now. Some times it makes no difference what area a mother is involved in, when it comes to them issues becoming apparent at home, as your family will not always be open to the support they would receive from you. I had worked years in advice and counselling, on issues relating to sex education and was open to be approached by my children. I had books, videos, and other information and had done numerous pregnancy tests. I must admit it has left me feeling somewhat angry with her for the added stress she had put on herself and the rest of the family. Even more reason for me to also have a life of my own.

King is a little better and has gone with his brother to his relatives in country. I spent a little while at his mum's yesterday and plait her hair. She was so nice; she cooked some dinner for me. She is worried about the way King has difficulty with his love pains. It is a little worrying, but girl, they all have trouble with the love issue, which is why the Queens and royal families have to hold on to their thrones. Jah knows.

I also phoned my friend yesterday, you know my sex partner, as I wanted to release the love pains that I had been feeling for King. I feel such a great presence within me that my thoughts are taking me to places that I have never been before and it has put a fear with my soul. Something is there and I am finding it hard to deal with. This power is consuming me and I cannot control it. I need to let go in order to find out what it is. I have prayed for an answer but do not see it (Or do I dare to see what is already there within my soul) Can it possibly be true? I had had no success in blotting out that kind of possibility but my soul keeps flying so high that I cannot reach myself.

Well I made sure that I let go and the truth came to me. I was angry about it yet suddenly wanted it to be so very much it hurt. I wish I had never went with Cliff especially while my soul is grieving for King, I missed him so I cried, I wanted to talk with him so I cried, but I suppose it will continue to happen right now as I know I have lost him. Jah, I am lost too. Have I the right to ask you to guide me again? What have you done to me Jah? Why do I offer my love, only to be left on the shelf with my grieving broken heart for sale? Do you not love me like you did before? Why have you allowed my womb to conceive again while I grieve for what I cannot have? Am I to be stone Jah? You and I both know that he does not want me.

Although I do not know what will become of my soul as I grieve over what will not be, somehow I know I will be alright, as at least Jah has still shown me my hearts desire and will aid me in the love that I feel growing and forming within me, although I can hardly cope with what I see and cannot even reason over it until I come to terms with what has happened to me first. Being in another mans arms however, brings at times comfort for those of us that cannot have what we truly desire. Not something I would encourage, as there are moments when this kind of choice may backfire as this one did for me.

I felt so cheap and empty after my sexual episode, although at the time it felt all right. I could now barely deal with the disgust at what I had taken part in. I should not have done it while my soul is in turmoil and no longer has peace. I just fear what is to come of all that I know is within me. I cannot say that King and I will ever become what I see; only Jah can bring that. He has brought me so much already, dare I even pray that a one would want a Queen with such a package to bare. I so crave to completely love him, but would he dare to love me? Even with what I have discovered. How on earth, can I show him what has happened between us? What will it do to him considering what he is going through already? How can he love me now when he couldn't love me then? I am so fed up with this loneliness that consumes me. I have to lay dormant with what I hold and pray that the time will come for the both of us to over stand the reality that we have to face now, be it together or apart. Only time will tell.

So until the next time.

Queen.Irena

Sela

10.LOVE IS A SPIDER'S WEB
Emails to a Queen
The Lonely Cave

Queen Imani

The spider has spun and spun so much over the last few weeks; I can't believe it has been so long since I have written.

Going away was a good thing for me as I had time to chill, and to spend quality time with Malachi after the stress that he had been facing. It is so hard for him to express his feelings about all that is going on for him. He is big for his age and is also going through puberty, so any number of things could be on his mind. Most prominent are the suicidal feelings that he now has. He smashed his computer along with printer and monitor. As for his CD/cassette player and his musical keyboard (Beyond repair) I fear for his safety to the extent that I cannot let him out of my sight for very long. Admittedly, this along with all my other ailments had taken its toll on my being, therefore bringing my feelings closer to that of Malachi's.

Having said that, Malachi had at least managed to express some of his feelings and is beginning to show signs of happiness again. He has been through so much lately. He had a session with a Psychiatrist who have assessed that I need support from social services. Malachi's autism seems to be a factor in his actions, particularly during the transition of puberty so I will certainly aid them (As always) in their search for the types of resources they could contact on my behalf. I am not the slightest bit ashamed to ask for support from anyone, as my family's safety is all that I have right now. I had contacted them a number of times for support in the past, but due to my possible directness or definite blackness, I still remained unsupported by them. I empathise with those who lose their children through suicide and grieve for the children that are neglected until it is too late for them.

I called Omar to ask for his support with the care of Malachi but he could only rejoice in my (so called) failure to maintain order amongst the children. He has expressed to them that he will live to see my downfall, so maybe this is what he was hoping for in way of support for his children. I had heard nothing from him regarding anything at all, so I will end the subject on him and begin another.

For the past few weeks I have been bleeding a lot, around four weeks now, and my body is worn out with it. It seems that the Coil had failed me, both as a means to reduce heavy periods and also as a form of contraceptive. I conceived King's baby, but my body gave it up as soon as it started. I was unwillingly aware of this fact and was reduced to secrecy due to the timing i.e. with the support that Tsion needed with her traumatic pregnancy and Malachi's delicate situation, which was more urgent, then anything in the world to me.

I had also taken on a major project besides everything. A family cultural event that was about to take place, involving members of the community that would entertain in order to empower the black community, had my name all over it. Yes, I organised it, directed it and obtained support to finance it. This was to be the first major event that I had become involved in.

The present experiences that I have been going through within my personal life, (Which included with my children), are also the first. I am in such a spin with so little time for myself that I feel I might just collapse with madness.

Constantly on my mind is King and the fragile condition he is in, although I had made attempts to make him aware of the pregnancy, he does not seem to be able to pull himself out of the pain he is in, to focus on what is happening to me. All I can tell him when he asks why I am sick is "I am bleeding a bit too much" I may well have been wrong, but I am sensitive too. Especially to the fact that with love in my heart for him and the loss of his baby, I had to cope with his rejecting my love knowing that I was carrying a life that I truly desired, because that life had already formed. He might merely have wanted the baby and not me. I think it might well had left me in another state of complete emptiness.

I feel that I am almost at that state right now with all that is in my life but continue in a robot like state until I find snippets of time to cry and grieve for the pain within my soul. When I carried my children this had been so. I was still alone in my role as a parent. Is my life to be so always Jah? It Seems I have never been in the right place at the right time.

I have been fighting with my feelings for King, one day up and the other down, but my love for him has remained strong and without doubt throughout. I think of him all the time now but will not peruse him for more than a friendship, as I do not want to lose what we have.

49

I do not feel unworthy of more, its just that I do not expect that someone can love me in the way I know I should be loved, with or without me as the mother of their child. The relationship that I have with King (Even with his rejection of me as his intimate love) still remains strong. He still holds me and cares deeply for me. He is attentive to the needs of both my children and myself, but he cannot love me completely as he would be wondering if he had made a mistake. I have my own opinion about that, but if I tell him he would not believe me. We make our choices in life and we make mistakes. King does not like to fail and is hurt with himself more than anyone when he has failed. Yes, I pray for his soul too.

My relationship with Tsion is limited. I am not in the mood for negativity so I am leaving her to her own devices. She is the fortunate one right now with all the support networks around her that I had also orchestrated and forced upon her. All she does now is just eat, sleep, and hide herself in her room, while all around her tend to her needs. I for one do not have the slightest bit of sympathy for her. I have my own grief to face, but will aim to continue to rekindle my royalty whether it is completely alone within my cave or not.

More soon

Jah Jah

Queen Irena

11. LOVE IS A SPIDER'S WEB

Emails to a Queen
Sacrifice

Greetings Dear Queen Imani

I pray that all is well with you on receiving this email. It has been a while since I wrote to you regarding my spider's web. As you know, with the Family Cultural Event being a complete success. What a joy it is to see families spending quality time together while they consume good home cooked food. At the same time, I have been up to my eyes. As for my personal life and love, there is always a story to tell to a Queen that can over stand it (At times).

Well I have been feeling many emotions that are not easy to explain. First of all, I have been a little overwhelmed with knowing what to do with Malachi as he has been with me a lot. Although there are supportive brothers and sisters around me, there are also times when only I can ease particular pains that are present for Malachi. He is so precious and delicate that even his laughter means much more. Now he is in much better spirits and is talking about his feelings more. He talks with King a lot and asks for him all the time. Thank God he feels able to ask for what he needs at times, and thank God that King is receptive to this. King had given Malachi the opportunity to express what is happening to him by letting him know that he can phone him at any time, so when King is due to come round, Malachi is waiting at the door. It looks funny and a little frightening, just in case King does not show. I think of the amount of children awaiting their fathers, for a day of fun that never happens. The kicks, bruises, scratches that are endured by the mothers that have to prise their children from the windows during the early hours, don't even get talked about here, even though I think of you too, Jah bless you.

As for Omar, well he has not been in the picture for anyone at all, and good luck to him too. I keep getting calls from someone that would hang up when I pick up the phone. I know it's him. He had not responded to the fact that his son had been going through a hard time, although I have shown him how much Malachi needs him. I am a little sad regarding the coldness he had shown by not contacting him, but this is the reality of the Livity that Omar has decided to troud. It throws me into utter bewilderment as to how on earth I could have been so wrong about him. I must go on though.

Tsion is a little better and is beginning to act in a more positive way. She is 20 weeks pregnant now and is finally starting to show. I try to be excited for her so that she can be a little more encouraged, but it is hard for me with what I had both been through alone, and with what I am feeling right now. I had spent a good two years in counselling sessions with Tsion to support her release of the pains she had held on to. She has remained closed while her brothers awaited my complete stimulation toward them. I had become many things in my life, yes, even an Octopus.

There is no relationship between Omar, Tsion and Marcus. He continues to slander Tsion's name within the community, telling all that she is a whore like her birth mother and myself. Marcus of course being the eldest son would not have it. This merely aided Omar to be true to himself, an absent father amongst other things.   It is so sad. Yet again here are two beautiful children, abandoned by their birth mother, now their birth father.

As you know I have been responsible for Tsion since she was six years old along with her brother Marcus from the age of five. It is not surprising that they do not feel able to become open to me regarding personal issues faced by them. If only they could overs the purity I hold within my heart for them. If only they overed that I even stayed with their father longer because Tsion would have left with him in the early days if we parted. Marcus was still in Jamaica at the time. I know she would have ended up dead from his neglect of her, as he only seemed to communicate with her when he wanted errands run. Little did I know that when I had left to nurse my mother through her sickness, he had left her to care for her brothers while he had pleasures with other women. She never told me then as she was stuck in her own version of 'He loves me, he loves me not'.

Those days were the hardest for me. Those were the days when he beat the children in order for me to do what he wanted. Those were the days when sex was the only intimate contact between us; of course he always wanted it. I would have been so happy just for the loving touches that I needed so much, but of course there was never any time for that. You know the coo, who could come to my room to rescue me from my plight before I could rescue myself from the oppression I had allowed him to have me in. With that over, time to move on with the now.

King and I, well we are not an item as he feels he should be available for his soul mate he has waited for over the last nine years. How I feel about that is very hard to express, as you know that deep in my heart I love him and keep thinking about him. It hurts so much that I feel that I am being haunted by it.

I do not bother go to his place in the evening much now. I see his mum during the day when he is at work. Its not that I don't want to see him sis, its just that I don't want him to feel that I am chasing him and just in case I start feeling that I have to see him to feel better. He says that, if he didn't meet Jane, things would be so different between us, but he has to follow his heart. I suppose he is being honest, but I don't know how I am meant to respond to that comment. It certainly cannot aid me in the recovery following the loss of his baby nor the physical effects that I am to face in the following months to come. Worst of all, it will never repair this broken heart. I am too old for this shit, especially after what I had experienced already. Somehow though he still provided care and respect towards me the best way that he could. He had been continually willing to spend whole days caring for the boys at his place and even pampered Tsion with his support to her as a warm daughter who also shared her sadness about her life with him.

While I was plaiting his hair on Sunday, we were able to talk about our feelings on the pregnancy issue and he ask me how I really felt, so I told him that I loved him deeply and that it is hard to explain it to him knowing that his love is for another. Somehow I know that he is still a little confused about me, as he is finding it hard to turn off his feelings for me. (What a mess) you might be thinking. It's not really a mess but it is certainly a situation that I never expected to happen. Having said this, no matter what has happened between us, he is still there for me.

We have our own ideas about what Men really want when it comes to love. We also know what it is like for us women as we always come to the point about our love, as it is so deep. I say this because I also have strange feelings that this other love does not love him in the way that he is dreaming and that she will hurt him badly, but he will have to find it out for himself. I do not want to be around him when this happens to see him suffer the rejection. We know what happens to the good men that get hurt in this way, but he seems to think it will be ok.

Some time ago, he felt totally torn between his feeling for me and her and was afraid of making a wrong choice. He had spent many sleepless nights wondering what to do about the love that he felt for me and even asked me what he should do, so there is a doubt there and I know it is not about me or him, it can only be about her, so only time will tell. In case you are wondering, I would never say choose me, as he alone must know.

With all of this, I do not think that feeling as I do for him is hindering us from having a friendship; it is just so deep at times, that I need to meditate a great deal. Sometimes I cry deeply for this love that I hold, as there seems to be nowhere that I can express it. At times, I feel like a silly child who cannot take no for an answer. I am definitely too old for this shit.

Turn in to the next session of "Love is a Spiders Web"

Queen Irena.

12. Love is a Spider's Web
Emails to a Queen
Duties Call

Queen Imani

I am a little concerned regarding the emotions that come up in this book as it may read distressing to you with the amount of issues that you may also be facing. I know life is not easy for you either and that although you have fewer children than I do, I know that the troud of a Queen is the hardest. I say that because no matter what we go through and what we face, we maintain our royalty, but carry a doubt about realising it because it seems so high. Girl, let me tell you, love overcomes all, as without maintaining the royal status I do not think I could even survive. (This may well be an opening for your own book as it is our time now).

I am getting ready to reason with Erran who I kept at home today. He is a little over the top of late so, He has become very angry and fights to have power over his brothers as well as over me, so we will have some time out to overcome the difficulties that we are having. He expressed his wish to live with his father because he gives him £5 a week and that he hates his twin. How the hell am I going to deal with this one Jah? Queen, you know the family ethics I am on regarding twins. Even more then that are the ethics on games regarding favourites between children and their fathers. Considering all though, I am so proud of the efforts made by both Arran and Erran as they have continued to work hard towards their goals in school along side the hard times they experience. Their wills to be are the strongest I have certainly seen; they beat like the Drums in my heart therefore set my pulse racing anytime I feel their pain. I pray they will accept my extreme love of them and not keep pushing me away; they strive for better with all their might but feel so frustrated with life.

I went to Malachi's parent's evening last night, which was great. It seems through all the worries that Malachi has had; he has continually worked hard in school and has reached many targets. Blessing his soul for the strength he holds within. I am so pleased for him.

I went with Malachi to King's so I could attend a meeting with his mum. My phone rang regarding Erran's behaviour so I had to leave Malachi and dash back home. Erran was not happy that Arran would not help him tidy their bedroom. He was calling Nathan (My youngest) names that Arran objected to; Erran wouldn't stop so Arran punched him. Erran got a knife and run after Arran. Tsion got the knife away so Erran got another knife and went for Tsion. She twisted his hand so Erran ran outside into the front of the house shouting child abuse.

I got home, got Erran in and gave him a piece of my mind (What a pleasant expression), then drove like the wind in my wildness to Omar's yard to knock him out for the distorted love that he had toward his children which aided them in their treatment of one another. Luckily he was not in although he might of been, as the way I rung the bell, I don't think I would have opened my own door if someone held onto the bell in that way.

I drove with Erran back to King's house, sat with his mum while he had Erran in his room to get to the bottom of what started his rage. Malachi was with King's brother Ian. Ian went to get food for the boys and then it was mum's turn to ask Erran questions regarding his behaviour. It was obviously difficult for Erran to cope with his feelings regarding his father, so talking with someone other then his family helped him today. The talking helped us all to cool down before we left, so King came home with us for a while and played with the children. Jah only knows how enlightened I am with this kind of care.

King says he needs to write before he can sleep but he was not able to express what he needs to write. We talked a long while and he lingered about the front door after we held each other then we said our goodbyes. Girl he really has a problem with this spider's web that he is stuck in. I don't really know what it is, but there is something. Maybe he has not let his love for me go and he cannot handle it right now. Even when I went to the gym this week to work off a few pounds and mixed up feelings, I noticed that King was acting a little strange. He seemed so confused when he saw me. I just got on with my usual thing, but he could not function, you know what I mean? I told him it felt strange for me seeing him so that he could open up, he asked why. I said it was because I had seen him a lot out of the university and that I had not been to the gym for a while. You and I can see that, but King denied there was anything strange about his behaviour. Well, it just shows how much men really deny their feelings. He kept looking over and was shy etc.

Erran has just come for his lunch and is getting ready for his reason with me. This is quality time that I need to have with him now. I take time out with each of the children according to their needs, but it is not always possible or convenient. There are times when the quality time out is urgent, as I am aware that even the school would have a bad day if yet another troubled soul (One of mine) attended school. I am doing the school a favour while giving much-needed time out. They are so different on a one to one.

So I will sign off here and continue in the next part of "Love is a Spiders Web"

Queen Irena

13. LOVE IS A SPIDER'S WEB
Emails to a Queen
Male Friends

Greetings Dear Queen Imani

I pray that this contribution to my book will reach you in the best of health and that Jah is keeping you and your royal family safe. This Web is still spinning and the almighty father (the Spider) has not finished with the works that are at hand.

I met a young man in the laundry by the name of Jason. He is a studio engineer (His words). We reasoned a little and I gave him my details. I want to get both King and Tessa to use the studio to get their songs recorded. I am not sure if Jason would be able to help them, but at least he can advise them. He seems nice enough.

When Jason came round, we reasoned for a long while. He talked about his love loss and other things. He seemed a bit needy, to the extent that he asked me for condoms. Well I told him that we don't need to use any. I just had to be decent and not cuss him (Poor ting) He went into the safety element and the rest, but I told him that I had no problems about people needing to be safe. I also told him that he did not need to be concerned about us (Might have been better to cuss him) as nothing was going to happen between us. It took a while but he went. It's a shame when men feel that they need to bring the sexual issue up before a woman has a chance to know them as it really spoils that relationship from remaining true.

Earlier that day King came round to reason with me. We were deep into our reasoning when his mum phoned, as she wanted to see me (She does at times). King was not pleased but went to get her. She stayed and done a little chatting with me, which was great. King was down stairs playing with the children, and then they both left. We (King and I) continued our reasoning by txt. Great fun.

Yesterday I went to see Tessa in her play at the theatre royal she really made the show and everyone loved her. This made me feel even more determined to get her to the studio. (King said he would give her some of his songs for the session). While I was at the show Erran was being cared for by King. I tried to get Jason on his mobile while I was out as the children let me know that he came and said he needed to talk with me. I didn't get him. I hope he is not hoping to start any games with me.

When I phoned home (while thinking of my sweet King) who answered? KING. I couldn't believe it. I thought I must have called his home instead so I acted as if expecting him to answer only to find that it was my home I had called. He told me that Erran was back and that he was waiting for me to return to reason with me, so much that he wanted me to hurry to him. Believe me Queen, I wanted to hurry too but you know something, I took my time, as I knew in his voice that he was willing to wait for hours.

I got in and he had spent the whole evening (on returning Erran) at my yard with the children. We went into the front room and had a very deep reasoning about this unique love that has happened between us. We also talked about the baby that I had conceived. He had been grieving but was unable to talk about it. The doorbell went and I instantly knew it would be Jason due to the lateness. My oldest son returned to announce that Jason had come and had asked for me, Surprise.

He came with CD's in his hand like he was staying some time, so I told him at the door that I would contact him later today as I was busy. I most certainly was not going to give up the special time I was having with King so, I made it clear to Jason that I did not have time for him at that hour. It was much too late to allow him to come into my home. He left with his tail between his legs. No really, he even walked like it was there.

After talking about how safe and loved and guided he feels by my love, he explained how he has never been loved in this way before and that it is important to him. He said that he thinks of me and then finds himself having a txt conversation with me, or I would phone him or that I would visit him or his mum or he would visit me. I showed him that I felt exactly the same. I told him about Jason, and what I think he now wanted from me. I also told him that he better get his songs ready as I wanted to make sure that Tessa got use of at least one song. I thought of how Jason was acting towards me but was not about to degrade myself with him to get that though.

This morning Jason came back to say that he was sorry about his behaviour the other night, and that he was lonely and the rest. I told him that it was not a problem with me, as I would not take advantage of him, so we could start the friendship again with a better over standing.

As you can see there is a lot happening other than keeping up with the madness in the house like, where is all the food that I bought for nearly £200 last week? Why is your room so messy? I left food in the pot to eat, why did you throw it away? Why doesn't anyone ever put a new toilet roll in the bathroom? Get out my room; you want me to beat you up, don't you? I will soon take some money out of my safe for you.

Other than the above Jah still dwells.

Queen.

14. LOVE IS A SPIDER'S WEB
Emails to a Queen
Soul Reflections

Greetings Dear Queen Imani

I pray the almighty father is with you, as he is with me, carrying me through the good and the bad times.

I would first of all, like to big up your presence and your patience in the untangling of this almighty Web that father has spun around me.

You see Jah has given me so much love to deal with at one time, that I sometimes wonder if he has nothing better to do with his time, but to play with my soul. At times my head is in a complete spin and I feel like a fly that has got caught in the Web waiting to be eaten. This does not happen, to my surprise, as father comes again and saves me by helping me to use my love differently to break free.

On Monday, Malachi, my youngest and I, were in the government office (you know what I mean). Malachi spotted Omar and we went over. (It pays to always make sure one is clean and shocking at these times). Omar could not make himself known to his 3 year old son who blanked him. We left.

Talking with someone on the road, Omar caught us up. He tried to hold Nathan's hand, but he became very upset so we went off. What a judgement the almighty has put his son on. Omar was at one time blessed with a Queen that showed him true love, but he threw it all away. I have no regrets regarding the end of my

64

marriage and will not hesitate in dealing with true love that is shown to me as this is what I happen to be thriving on. Talking of true love.

My sweet King came over the same Monday evening with his brother. We chatted a bit then they got up to leave while the doorbell rang. We opened the door and surprise, it was Jason. I introduced him to my people and they left, leaving Jason in the company of Nathan and myself.

I noticed that King did not hold me as he usually did before we parted. It felt wrong so I had in mind to challenge him on this as nothing is supposed to get in the way of the friendship love that we share together. Our hug had become a non-verbal agreement.

Jason played some of his music to me. Girl, he has talent. We had a good reason about his music and I told him about Tessa and King that would like to meet with him to further their songs. He was happy with this and showed me that his aim was to finish his studio and work with artists in the area. It was a good evening, much better and more open than the last one with him.

This day seems to be rather long, does it not? Well after the "Go to your bed" and "Your school clothes ready for the morning" bathing my baby, (always the most fun) as he is in his element in the water. Getting him to sleep is nice, because he rubs my face while he falls asleep, and I continually kiss him.

I had to make a call to you know who. King and I reasoned on the possibilities of putting music to his songs etc. I asked him why he failed to hold me before he left. He said, "It was him, Jason, he was there". I left him to think about what he had just said but did not pursue it. I wondered if it was a thing that men would normally do or was it because he did not want Jason to see us hold each other, because of other feelings that he had not dealt with.

Went to the Gym on Wednesday after visiting mum. Mum is so down and it was hard to make a conversation with her. In fact, it was a little worrying to see her like that. I talked with King who seemed a little fed up with the depression his mum is in but understood that she may be going through the Menopause. (I don't remember my mother having this experience) He sits with her at times like this but as she doesn't want to worry him she would not open to him. We had a good reason about his feelings on this and I left.

On Thursday I dropped some shopping drop off at King's yard, worked with his brother on his CV and then was able to really reason with King. This turned out to be one of the best moments that I have had with my sweet King. Jah knows it was wonderful.

I say that the reasoning with King was one of the best times spent with him, but there had been many moments that have been special, warm, inspirational and just full of power, but Thursday, we laughed together, we chatted, and we talked about his movement towards his plans with his songs. This was great as his song writing talent is exceptional. His songs describe emotions felt not only by him, but also others that had experienced all the pains around him in the spiritual sense (if you know what I mean). Reading his songs leaves me alone with my feelings, within the walls of a large golden cave filled with a warm energy force that only he can possibly over stand or explain.

We talked about my sexual partner Cliff and the txt I sent to him. I explained to King that I needed passion and care. At the same time, I felt a need for my sexual desires to be fulfilled knowing that Cliff could help me to quench this thirst. He asked me what came of the txt. To tell the truth, I had not bothered to pursue this area, as I did not get a response from Cliff. King suggested I should call him to find out what had happened. I decided to do that.

I happened to mention Winston as he had replaced a CD player that was stolen (another story, there are so many) from my home. King's reaction hit me like I had just been shot. Girl, he said he remembered that I had mentioned Winston before and that he would like me to tell him the story about him. I told him that the man sometimes called me his Queen and would occasionally give me gifts and also say things like, "I would go to the end of the earth for you, kiss your feet"......... and so on. My reaction to these comments, have always been to change the subject. I do this, as I see Winston as an elder that I respect and value as an important source of knowledge and over standing.

King suggested that Winston was merely reflecting on my soul which he had seen through me eyes (its that bloody eye liner isn't it). I had never taken the time to see this in relation to Winston. It put a fear in me that sent my head in a spin. We spent some time on this issue, as King felt the need to point out that the man was knocking at my door and that he wanted me. I blushed and tried to hold the thought but my whole being began to fear an elder on my tail. I say this because of my ethics on elders as a forbidden fruit and of course my past abusive experiences with them. I just cannot go there and have no want in that area. This was not a an act of disrespect or rejection of him on my part at all, as he had not disrespected me but had supported me with activities for my children. He is a good man. There had just not been a thought in that area. I left after seeing that mum was all right.

Later that evening I phoned Cliff to find out what was happening. I asked him about his lack of response to my messages. He said he was shocked to get such a txt a week after my explaining that I had miscarried a Baby for someone I had fallen in love with. I had to explain that this period of time had passed and that although I was healing from the painful impact it had on me, I still feel very deeply for King, but I was learning to love him differently, which totally fulfilled my spiritual being. I also showed him that I was left with a sexual desire that needed to be met, which, if pursued by me, towards King might destroy the relationship that we now had. I did not intend to put that at risk. I showed Cliff that both he and I know that he could provide me with the passion I needed, and that I didn't need to explain the passion that he would experience from me in return. Cliff explained that he would like that, but needed some time to clear his slate first as he had to be in one piece to begin a deeper experience with me. I won't hold my breath and wait for him to recover from what he had heard. I just had to talk with you know who again.

Sometimes I wonder why I feel drawn to him in this way. Do I love him more than I should? Sometimes the last thing I think of before I sleep is King and that first thing I think of when I awake is he. I get angry with myself at times as I dream of him making passionate love with me, but this makes me feel empty. When I see him after these dreams, I feel better as I receive a more powerful and sweeter love from him in a spiritual sense before all other avenues and suddenly I don't feel out of my depths.

I have never looked at Love as being a spider's web until King came into my life. He never pressures me and is attentive to me, but is stuck toward me as I am toward him. I know this relationship we have is rare and exceptional, but I also know that in order for us all to manage to live with true love, we need royal people like King walking with us. He has opened a part of my being that I had locked away inside of me for so long. He has aided me in the refurbishment of my soul in a way that I can only pray never to lose. He is the best Man that has ever happened to me. My sweet soul brother, companion and King.

Blessings on you, your King and Princes
Jah's love endures forever more. Rastafari lives.

Queen.Irena

15. LOVE IS A SPIDER'S WEB
Emails to a Queen
Lets Get to the Point

Greetings.
My dear Queen Imani.

What a lovely day it is out there. I pray that the rays given to I by the Most High sun are blessing you. Praising the Most High.

I know this next excerpt has been eagerly awaited but what the heck, it's good to wait sometimes.

I decided to reason with Winston but first of all I called him to ask a few questions. I asked, "When you had the tapes you gave to me made, was the music on your instruction?" he said "Yes" I continued, "When did you have them made?" I waited for a reply, and then asked again. "About a year ago." he said. Well I just had to ask "Why did you give them to me?" He laughed and said, "Well, you will have to work that one out for yourself". I got mad and told him he had better come round for a more full reasoning because "You men make me sick. You are always on a mystery trip so that women have to be wondering about your actions. I am not on that, I am upfront, so I want a reasoning with you as soon as possible, ok bye". I hung up. I was not angry with him; it's just that he is a family man, old enough to be my father. I don't want him to be misled by my resurfacing or by my sexuality showing. He seems to drop by at any time and calls to say he is on his way expecting me to be in.

He came about two hours later. Winston had been showing my boys how to do some gardening around the local church. I had become strongly involved in the management of the link between the children and school holidays (by Winston's request) this meant a lot of meetings with Winston over the past seven months. At times I felt the work involved over bearing. The meetings became so regular that I used to dread Winston ringing the doorbell. I know I could have withdrawn my involvement, but girl the Play Schemes help me to get some peace during the holidays from my children and it is Winston who cares for them at these times, so I suppose it is out of respect and also to oversee management of a great service for both my family and for others in the community, as to why I had became involved.

Tsion made Winston some food and we went into the front room to overs what was going down. We first of all talked about the summer school business and then he went into his critique of reasonings. He said, "Sometimes a one can reason over so much, the issue gets mashed up." I waited a while and asked, "Is this what I think it is?" (Who said it were only white people that went red, if I was black until I was blue, the redness would still show through the skin on my face). He continued. "You see this is not an essay that you need three thousand words for, it's just plain and simple. You don't even realise the capacity of the impact your personality has on people. You just go around and blam der so and blam der so". He continued. "You are a Queen that gives off certain energy forces that makes every one feel safe and proud to be a part of something that you are a part of."

71

I was able to stop him by telling him that I had realised that this quality was within me many years ago but was also aware that my husband was afraid of this so had done everything in his power to imprison me so that no one else could see, especially his friends in high places. I continued to explain that he himself had been able to see this in me because the most high had set me free so my soul was open for the world to take note. I told him that, there were now people in my life including him that had taken the time to care for my children and myself. This could not be possible with their father around in the state that he was in. He made sure all the good ones stayed away or visited him when I was away.

I also showed Winston that, I loved and respected him as an elder that provided me with the wisdom and support that was needed by me and that in return I had given him support in both his and my ambitions within the community, however I could not and did not want to move into an intimate or sexual experience with him.

He hesitated, then said "Well I am not talking about a sexual thing as when I need that, I can get that. This is higher. From the time I met you and especially when you talk. Don't you notice, when you talk every one listens to you?" I butted in "Yes but" he butted in "No you listen" I kept my mouth shut and tried to keep my ears shut too but it didn't work. "I have the utmost respect for you and I would walk to the ends of the earth for you. You have a light that shines."

I felt like crying. I feel so deeply that this was true but it is so frightening as this is what happens, people fall in love with me and sometimes I fall in love with them.

The only thing is I know that I am true but it is not always clear if they are true. I suppose I have to keep working on myself in order to find out who it really is with the help of the Most High, Please Jah.

I sat quiet; "Anyway" he sensed the vibes and said. "What country do you want to visit this year?" Here we go again! He has not accepted what I said has he? Neither has he got to the point.

Tune into more of this "Love is a Spiders Web"
Queen

16. LOVE IS A SPIDER'S WEB

Emails to a Queen
Swollen Heart

Hi Dear Queen
I have been thinking of you out there hustling and a bustling, through the heavy traffic and people in your face. Sis I am out there too and so are all the others. We barely have time to take a stop and make that call to a soul sister or brother just to say hey Jah Jah. The ones we do see in our travels are too busy to do so just as we are at times. It is almost as if we are now computers, able to predict what will happen next so no need to reason.

I feel a little low today, the vibes are not right. The day started off with the usual two-hour wait at the doctors with Malachi as he said his feet were hurting. I know he was telling the truth, but what the hell. I also know that it is Thursday (swimming day at school for him) and he does not want to go. He cried last night and cried this morning so I was a little glad when he brought up the painful feet issue so the opening was made for us to reason. Malachi needs a complete uninterrupted one-one so he can open up. Only I seem to know how to question him to gain the clear response needed to carry him through the day's grace. I realise that if I were to lose this sweet child; I could never use a handbag again, as his bones would take his place. Jah please help him to see that I need him to be all right.

Malachi is finding growing up very difficult. For him to tap into his resources via male role models well, what

74

can I say? Omar has been around for most of his life but although he has spent time with him alone, he never liked answering difficult questions so a bond was not made. Omar never had a bond with his own father; therefore he had no model to work from and had not prepared himself to meet the needs that Malachi might have. I suppose at times, the mould is very hard to break when it comes to bad fathers. The relationship that Malachi and his oldest brother have is not complementary either, as there seems to be some animosity between them. There are certainly no warm glances between them. Maybe it's the attention I give to Malachi.

With no continuous focus from a male toward Malachi has left him without the guidance that every child needs for vital development towards manhood. It has been particularly difficult for him to find sense from the many changes that have happened to him both between his parents and it's effect, and also the physical ones due to puberty. He is easily mistaken for a man and his autism has not helped either.

It is all very well when a woman feels that a man is not needed to grow a good boy, but a mother cannot teach her son how to be a man, she can only teach him how a woman must be treated. A mother that is in tune with the one within can only do this, the true one within. How can this be maintained if this mother is raising her children alone? This mother would not accept the distorted quality shown by the father of these children. I would rather go it alone to grow them.

The roads that we trod all come from the same foundation, with the man and the woman creating a one from within, through the woman. She has to show her children the truth, as she is her child's most high while the man is the child's almighty father that provides the complimentary wisdom and protective direction.

It is a strain having to sort for complementary wisdom and protective direction from those other than the father of my children. It has left me feeling sad and lonely (no not for him). It has left me with a swollen heart. This is not how I would have liked it to be. I have never felt that a child should grow without a father and have never wanted to bring my own children up alone. This may well be why I even stayed with Omar so long after knowing that he had so negatively affected the children with his treatment of me, but it had to stop sooner or later. I have made many mistakes along the way, as have countless others, but if I stop believing in the fact that I will never give up trying to find the true one within me, I know that many will fall. I have responsibilities that I have to face twenty-four hours a day. The most important one is to myself. That is to be free and to continue to receive and to give love in the way that I am supposed to and to be whom I know I am. Queen Irena.

Nuff respect

Jah Jah

Queen Irena

17.LOVE IS A SPIDER'S WEB

Emails to a Queen
Tapping with the Spirit

Greetings to you my dear Queen.

I am sending you my love and my continued experiences of understanding the Web of the Spider, The most high. This is an awakening transition.

Firstly I spent the weekend in a state of total empowerment whose foundations lay within the high priestess' queens, empress' Kings, Princess' and princes in my life and within those that do not yet oversee the true meaning or concept of Royalty.

The reasoning between King and myself on the evening of my last excerpt (Friday) inspired me. I had been feeling down and had sent a txt to him to warn him of my imminent visit. I needed to be in his company. He always instantly had time for me and I also took it for granted now and then. Today I felt so needy (You know the feeling).

It was, as it is at times, difficult to express without letting go of my deepest feelings and my needs of love, care and support. You see, the fact that King has been able to (or should I say) I allowed him to, see into the depth of my being, he had been given guidance towards his own issues of troubled love. This, although not a new experience, had taken its toll on my soul due to the issues in my own life and of course because of the love that I also felt for him. No, don't be alarmed! He has given me guidance too, the kind that has opened me to the effect that I have on those around me whether it be my children or the men (or should I say) man that King proclaims to be, my soul mate.

I hesitate as I even type, as this is such an emotive topic for me. I also hesitate because the man (Winston) and I are to have a meeting soon, so he will be knocking at the door at any moment. There is so much to say that I wouldn't mind if he never shows. Its not that I don't like' him, its just that he is around a lot and seems to be in a spin himself for what ever reason. I just need to have a laugh.

I had a good dance to some old Barry Biggs. What great memories of school days. I decided to be open to Winston in order that he could express what he truly wanted from me when he arrived.

King says that I am not being clear about what I want and I am not being fair about what my children need. I got defensive about that. I feel I had sacrificed a great deal of myself with my aims to provide the love and care needed to bring forward all the children, even with regards to the pretence of continually showing respect to Omar who never respected me. I taught my children how to respect their father even though they knew he was always in the wrong in his treatment of me. I have always shown love to those around me and had received love in return from all except Omar.

Why then should I give my ultimate love to a one that I do not feel for within my heart and soul? A one that is merely treating me in a way that he has no choice but to do, because of the respect that I have for myself. He is not the only one, there are others? There had always been others. Even during my days of commitment to

Omar. At that time they had not been rescued by the most high. As for me well I was too busy denying who I was then and continued to see myself as a non sexual being. They were like me, a fly stuck in the Web. I see Winston as a one in that situation. Waiting for the almighty spider to release him into my arms. He knows that he would be safe with me you see; the only thing is that I do not want him. I have no wish to be his prize at the end of a bad day at home with his family I want all or nothing but not with him. I have too much to give to get so little in return.

I seemed to have followed a pattern with the men in my life. A life where I had always chosen someone who either turned out to be with someone else or in love with someone else or a one that could not committee themselves to me. All this had done is kept me in a prison like state, always socialising alone or amongst my Queens. This is not to say that my Queens had not been there for me, Jah and they know how much I truly love the care they have given to me. I have not however, to date, felt that a one had shown completely contented with a walk with me or happy to show me the love that I desire from them. Not even content with time out with just me for a few hours away from all. Do I put some kind of fear in them? Is it my love that they fear? Am I too over bearing for them?

Winston showed me another side of him today. It seems he was looking for me to rescue him. I thought I had rescued him at the beginning of our meetings about seven months ago. He is quite able to do all the things within the community and more than I can do. He talked about the love less relationship that he is in. He couldn't even look at me. He talked about his reputation and not wanting to be seen walking around with women as he has people that know him within the community. He says he has his partner and children etc to think about. I do not remember asking him to explain anything. I am however sure that I am not looking to move around in secret. I want a one that is not afraid to walk with me and share with me. I have spent a lifetime locked up as a prisoner. I have been (as I said before) freed; give thanks to Jah for his pleasures in me. I was not surprised with what Winston had to say and was glad to hear it too.

I showed King that I had fear in releasing my ultimate love to anyone because of the experience of a backlash as being totally overbearing and that I would rather hold on to that part of my love. "What is it? He says". It was a little while before I could answer. He asked again and again. "It is everything, every part of me, the true one within." The reasoning took another turn.

Help me Jah, the spider is coming to consume me. I thought. "Is it anything to do with what happened with me, or did he say to me." I didn't hear all the words that he said clearly. I waited and hesitated; I didn't dare ask him to repeat. I said "No" he asked if I was sure. "Yes" I said and hesitated again, as I now overed what he had asked. I lied. Well maybe not lied, it really felt that when he asked that, everything was affecting me right then, even what happened to him and with him. It might be because it was so recent. I suppose I felt that I didn't give him all my love at the time, but on reflection I now think I did, but in a way that was completely different than it had been with anyone else.

"What are you afraid of"? He asked again. "I am afraid of my power, it's too much for me". Here comes another question. "Why" he asked. By then I was in tears, as to why. Well this was about the fact that I see the Most High when I am complete. No, I mean truly. When I call him he appears. When I am asked to explain this I am taken over in a way that leaves me unable to talk so I cannot explain. The one who asks has no memory of the question they just asked me. "Because the Most High is there," I replied. "Well that is where you should be, with him" he insisted. "I need time to repair. I am not repaired from all the hurt that I feel inside yet. It has taken me over and I have to control it." He just had to come back for more (I supposed I asked for it) "Why do you feel that you have to control it? You cannot control it. Just let go."

I went into my defensive mode again. I do this as I do not have any control over my body and if I told him what was happening to me physically it would blow his mind. He is neither ready nor do I feel he has the capacity to overs the reasoning as to why it must happen. I have not yet met a one who is on the level to overs my physical condition and the movement that I feel within me. I know this may sound a little or even widely abnormal but the most high has both the overs and is in control of what is to come so he is here with me while I go through, as well as when I reach the other side. I left to collect my children.

I spent a while in my travels reflecting on my life and on those that I truly love. There are so many, from school to the present day. Many have made such a positive impact on my soul, some not so positive.

I give thanks for the continued development of my spiritual being. Selah.

81

Queen Irena

Love is a Spider's Web" will be back soon

18. Love is a Spider's Web

Emails to a Queen
Protective Circle Force

Queen Imani

I pray these words reach you at a time when you are ready to experience the powers of the Most High. I am sending you my deepest and warmest blessings and protection through the transitions of this excerpt.

I am here after a mellow day preparing the children for a weekend of camping. Malachi, Nathan and I remained. I will miss the others, but Jah knows they needed to get away and I needed to have this weekend without any pressure on my soul.

Jason turned up before I could sleep. He brought a pair of trainers for Marcus (at his request) I thanked him and showed him that I was tired and going through spiritual awakenings. He said he would not stay long and said he would provide me with a tape deck so that I could listen to my tapes on another level. He had also brought me a wrist chain, which he put on me. What is the most high doing to me? Is he playing with me again? I didn't know what to say but I thanked him. He seems much better and is sweet with his nervousness.

Jason seemed nervous around me and constantly twiddled with his hair (that got on my nerves after a while) he seemed to be holding back from saying so much. I gave him room to talk. "I just want to prove I am a man of my word," he said. "I don't want you to prove anything to me, just be who you are and that is fine". I know it is because he showed me his weakness in the beginning. He feels a bit awkward. I am not going to keep reassuring him. He is a good enough man and will be all right and he is supposed to know it. I have no intention of showing him negativity. He will have to take me as I am. He continued. "When I reason with you I leave on a different level. I feel contented within myself and want to show you that I respect you for that. I just want to move forward and put my skills into practice." He started twisting his hair again. "You seem to be a little nervous, are you? Are you finding it difficult to reason with me? I asked him, Hoping he could explain. Yes. A bit, it's just that I am trying to move away from certain feelings and to get over what I have been through." I assumed he meant the sexual desires that he had towards me. "I feel negative towards women right now" he said. I was silent (I was not going to ask anything) he couldn't go on, so he said "Anyway I am going home to cook." We said our good byes and he left. I felt a little sad for him (no, not sorry) sad about the Kings and what we all need and lose. It certainly highlighted my own pain about what was happening in my own life.

It was hard to sleep that Friday night, but I managed a little. When I awoke on Saturday, I felt so tearful that I was on the verge of weeping all day. I suppose the space within me opened up more than I had expected it to. After everyone was up and all over the place, Winston called for Ezekiel and left him a card for his birthday. Winston is fond of Ezekiel as he is of Winston. This is very good for both of them and for me, as it gives me a chance to watch Ezekiel develop more independently of me. He is showing signs of breaking away from things mothers would want to talk about, and asking questions of a man in my life that is in need of a kind of bond new to his own experience. As for my bond with Winston, well he seems a little confused to me, as he gets tongue tied at times. I support him with his time with Ezekiel and my son is pleased, so I am happy for him.

My interest at that moment was the reunion that was on later. I told Winston about my Reunion of old school friends and that we were all forty this year. I asked Winston what he was doing later, as I wanted to go onto something else and to give him a chance to take me out, if he was interested. He told me of a party and where it was. "You can go if you want," he said. "What do you mean? I wouldn't mind going, do you want to go?" I said. "No, No. I am not going." He replied. Did he just ask me out? Well I think Winston wanted me to be there but I got the impression that there might be friends of his there so his reputation would be at stake and that he didn't want to take me, or more to the point, he might well be pissed that I did not want a relationship with him (I am getting too old for this shit) he couldn't look at me and left soon after. That felt a bit strange but nothing was going to stop me from where I really wanted to go out. I still felt a little tearful from Friday but made myself feel better by making sure that I cooked a good meal for the children so they would behave well for their sister (You know) a soul meal that would help them to sleep well and give me a chance to have a good time, as that was my intention.

I got a call from Lela. A Queen that always knew when my soul was opened as she opened too. She showed me that I was special to her and that I helped her to bring out the logic that aided her in her progression through her love experiences. I told her what I knew in my soul she needed to hear from me. The fact that she wanted to phone a lost love that had just used her (to mend his own broken heart) was merely part of the transgression she was on. (This she was aware of) She needed me to tell her in order that she could give herself the dignity to not call him. We do this for each other, as you know most Queens do.

Got another call from Queen Heart. My sweet queen, whom I love with all my heart and she is within my soul too, if I so much as utter a negative word, she would jump right in and remind me of my worth as she regarded me as a woman of essence that shines for the entire world to see. She was adamant that because of the love I have to offer, she was not happy to know that I had fallen in love so soon after Omar. Maybe she was not clear that it had been at least six years since I had fallen out of love with Omar. I had spent years trapped in the old philosophy that children need fathers' no matter what condition they were in. She had herself, become a prisoner by her partner and all the children that he had produced without her. Her love is so pure for them that they would eat her if she was food and still never notice her. I told her that I loved her, while thinking (I want my Queen back) please Jah Jah.

I called you, as you know my Queen Imani. You were able to show me that because of who I am, this was the reason why I had been experiencing the Web. You showed me that because I had been open many, had seen and was going through with me. I had the opportunity to share what I have in a way that could only lift me to where I needed to be. It had certainly aided in the preparation for the evening ahead so I wore my robes. I

Give thanks for that. May all you pray for, belong to you.

When I walked into the reunion, I felt like I just walked on the stage. I never heard so many call my name at one time. I saw those I hadn't seen for twenty-four years. Kisses everywhere and from everyone. What a blessing oh Jah. Having ten women kiss me just because they see and remember me for who I was then and for who I am now, the experience was better than an orgasm. Nothing was held back from them and nothing from me. At times we just sat and looked at one another and laughed and even screamed occasionally. We talked, showed each other old photos and we took new ones. The best of all was when we got on the stage and danced together. We moved with passion, love, happiness, excitement and total empowerment. We should have had a camcorder.

Thinking about the party that I was told about by Winston, I drove past the area. Slowly. I was aware of a voice within me saying don't go, it will bring to an end to the power you had experienced earlier. I listened to it and went home. Had a good sleep too.

Ezekiel's birthday was quiet. He had wanted to see his birth father. (That is not even the right name for him.) He was definitely there for the conception, but as for the five months I spent on bed rest, stitched up and laid up in hospital, hooked for the birth, there is a blank page. Ezekiel had managed to get a message to him so he returned his call. He had promised to spend time with Ezekiel during the next holiday. I will be there for him when he sees his father is not serious. If Ezekiel's father had changed, well, I will give thanks and pray to the one within for forgiveness.

Winston passed to tell Ezekiel of a gardening job where he can make some money for himself. He also talked to me about the party. "Did you go?" I asked. He skirted around the issue a bit then, "Yes I was there". He replied. (He really did not want to take me). "Anyway it was good." He went on. He could see by now I was not the slightest bit interested in his bloody party. He started talking about the play scheme so I shut off a bit. He left.

Ezekiel and Malachi spent the day with Omar. Before I left them, I had asked Omar for the money needed to help feed and clothe his seven children. He made it clear that he had none. I told him "You better sort yourself out and get some, because I will ask you again." He could not look at me. "Oh by the way", I said. "Make sure you do not degrade the children with the display of pictures of your daughter that you had when you lived with us. I see no photos of your children with me. Mind what you do and be careful or you might become ill. Bye." The children had witnessed him destroy our family pictures before I threw him out.

I got a call from Queen Selah. (Even more blessings). We had not reasoned for around a year. She said "I feel I need to connect on a deep spiritual level with a one who can over stand and can heal. There is no one in that category around me right now and I miss you I Queen." My heart missed a few beats. I responded. "Greetings my dear Queen, I have continued to send you spiritual vibrations while you appear before me with your blessed love and wisdom to guide me through my darkest and brightest hours. How merciful the most high is to show us the eternal depths of our being while sending the energy forces that has brought us back together again. I miss you too my sweet Queen. Rastafari."

Queen Selah had an insight into the kind of wisdom through love that always held me, as my insight did for her. The fact that we had not seen or held each other for over six years was not even an issue. We loved and provided for each other; spiritual guidance during very important times and that was it. Our words would float in the air and carry us if in a hot air balloon. The love is Pure, sweet and light as a feather, Selah.

I was lifted by the events of the weekend in a way that prepared me for the following weeks transition and all that it held for I through the watchful body of the Spider and its web.

As the forces are, more will be revealed in "Love is a Spider's Web" next time, so don't miss it.

Queen Irena.

19. LOVE IS A SPIDER'S WEB
Emails to a Queen
Red Day Blessings

Dearest Queen Imani.

I pray that you are well this evening. Haven't heard from you lately are you all right? I know that we will talk before you get this but it will be good for you to know that I was thinking of you and praying for you.

I am into the second day of this transition. (What happened to the first?) You may be thinking. Well as women all over the world would know, the first day is the day of recognition that Jah has given us the ultimate burdens. Firstly, with the over standing toward all that is within and all that must come. Secondly, the colour is Red for us all. No matter what Race we say we belong to. We have always been one. I love all you women who say you are not of my race because when the first day hits you, even though you know when it is to come you feel as I do. Do you want me to tell you how I feel? Well I feel hurt, I feel sad, I feel pain, I feel it running down, I feel sick, I feel mad, I feel a great love loss, I feel rejected, I feel just as you do on "The second day".

My sweet sistren Anne and my gentle Goddaughter Sally, had come for the weekend. It is a great joy to know that the almighty father has sent to me yet another guide to see me through this time. We have experienced great loss together and had been able to hold on to the faith within to bring life through our children and show the world that the most high had always been there for us. No, we could never grieve forever, so a live baby just had to be born to us, Jah be praised.

I became a Godmother to Sally five hours following my mother's death. I had been praying to my mother (The Most High) until she died to aid her in "The Pass Over". When I got home I sought support from Jack and received the maximum care from him (I give thanks to Jah for that). I was then off to become a Godmother for the first time in the same church that my mother attended and where she, a week later had a short history read by me to those gathered before her burial. There have been many episodes in my life, I realise now that I must frighten people. Do I frighten you my Queen? We will reason later.

While most of the children are away, It is warming to be around a one that can over stand many aspects of my life and relate it to her own transitions. I give thanks for her steadfast care and attention and pray that my Godchild Sally is blessed with her energy force.

I had a visit from Sweet King this evening. Gracious you are oh father, that you shower such blessings on me. I was heavily under the demands of "The second day" and just had my fifth bath of the day. He listened to me, and gave me his love expressions (I managed a little smile) but was upset as his mother had a bad Nosebleed. He explained about her blood pressure medication had not been taken by her. I felt it for him and explained the importance of the support she would need and related it to the experience faced by my own mother following her reduced blood pressure medication. I knew at times this Queen was adamant that she was all right and would not take any advice regarding her health. He over stood as he had decided to contact his other family members about it.

I felt a sudden pain and had to change again as I was now flooding badly. He looked at me and knew I was having a hard time so he made me a hot drink and showed me his usual tenderness. He said he would talk· with his relatives and be advised whether to call a doctor to intervene, because of not wanting more guilt pressure from her. I felt it was a good idea to talk with his family, and to reject the pressure that tempted him to hold onto guilt, so I told him this.

Before he left, we held each other tight in recognition of the feelings that we both had for her for me and for him. I felt warm in his arms and realised that at that moment, he was passing onto me the purest of his love that had been so needed by me during all my red days through the year. The kind spiritual love that goes way beyond any man made rules on you women stay over there until you are clean because you must now not be loved, seen, not be talked to, not to read the scriptures, not cook food for your people, not be stroked until you sleep (in your pain) and dare? I say Flying the Red flag. I wonder when a Queens worth will truly be over stood.

I give thanks to your royalty,
For recognising my love.
Your blessings have inspired,
Me to write the above.
My love endures.
Queen.
An adapted txt to my King,

20. Love is a Spider's Web
Emails to a Queen
Defensive Love

Dearest Queen Imani.

I have to say, that at this very moment, my heart feels like it is passing its last few drops of blood for the pain that I feel in my very soul right now. It hurts so much that I think I might just collapse while I reveal it all.

Tsion will be leaving us some time soon. I love her so much, but She is in need of her independence and is transcending on her way to becoming a mother, she is taking the first step. Well, my heavy heart on the one hand says, "You will be just fine". At times though, I feel so sad for her. She is a beautiful being, but she doesn't know it. She can give so much to her baby, but she is in need of giving it to herself first. She so needed her birth mother to love her but instead I am told (by her birth mother) that she cannot be there for her, as she no longer knows her daughter and that I must take her place. I pray for her (Tsion that is), and will always watch over her like the angel that she needs, but my life is here where I belong with the spirits that were planted within my body. You see Jah overs all. My children belong on a higher level that is like no other and I will be given the guidance in order to show them what they need to see in this time, forsaking all others, so if their fathers or mother (who clearly know what is to be), happens to be against the will of the most high, then they will lose all their children too.

I just got in from seeing my adopted head Queen (The mother of my sweet King). Firstly, I spent a great part of it with my Queen. Oh, we danced and talked. She looked so happy while she talked about her young days and her friends and her children and her life. I don't remember my mother telling me those things (well at least I don't remember the smile that would usually accompany it). I remember my mother, my head Queen Dowling. What a real Goddess to be remembered. Sometimes I miss my mother bitterly. I feel that right now as I imagine the love pains she must have had and wonder if we had had longer together whether she would have opened up to me and expressed what her love experiences were like.

My adopted Queen helped me to hold all the good things about my mother. (It was every thing about her). She had given me the chance to feel her again between my arms and just hold her again. I give thanks to the very most high for giving me these feelings with a wonderful woman such as my adopted Queen. I was able to dance with my mother and hold her in recognition of the love pains that she had and of the pains that are around for us all now. The only thing is that I cannot express how I feel towards her special son King. Not that I want to reveal too much.

She is so protective of him and his feelings and worries about his love pains, that she asked me not to tell him what I feel for him. It makes me feel boxed in with my emotions. It is so hard to get a balance. I truly desire to express all that I feel, but Jah and I know that I fear the repercussions especially if his soul is not able to accept me. If I do express to him and he rejects me again, the pain would be bad and she would know because mothers do (Know that is), we not only give birth to our children but also to a spiritual awareness of "knowing." More to the point, is the fact that there is the issue of his "soul mate" and not forgetting our friendship.

I have often felt deep within my soul that our coming together was not by chance. From the moment "The true one within" showed King's soul to me, I knew we were to be and that he was my "soul companion". I have never been confused about that fact. I had allowed everything to overpower what it all meant for him. I asked myself, why was it that we spent so much time together? I mean we met regularly and inspired each other; we had a great deal of over standing on the issues of love, yet both had held back on our love. Why? I can only say for myself that from the time King became distressed about the torn feelings he was experiencing in regards to his soul mate and myself, I began to withdraw from him even though it was extremely painful for me. It leads me to wonder why he had opened the door to me, let me into his heart and taken my love, only to allow it to tear him apart. I felt so responsible for his emotional condition that I reverted to the responsible woman that I sometimes am, and held onto the pain. (Why do we continually do that?)

I went to reason with King. I was not sure of what to expect. We had both had a hard week in various ways and had a great deal to overs on. I had been feeling totally alone and rejected, with the grief of losing both King and his baby. I felt that I had even assisted him with my rejection by not showing him what was happening to me. How could I have been so uncaring of myself? I have spent so many years caring for others, that I had forgotten that I needed care too. Its not that King had not cared for me, as he himself showed me that I should not have held back to protect him. He felt hurt that I had not involved him from the time I knew I had conceived his baby. He had no idea what that was like for me. He was ready to die because of how he felt, and I wanted him to live and be happy for us so I could tell him. I waited and waited for him, but he got further and further away from me. We never seemed to be in a situation where I felt I could show him what was happening. Both my Queen and King were so distraught that, well you know the rest.

I cried a lot during those weeks, alone at night I would set my alarm just in order to prepare myself for the pretence of being all right. When the bleeding started I thought it had been the episode I had had, with my sexual partner (I even did that to help erase my feelings for King), was it because I had not told King? Was it because I was doing too much? Was it because I loved him in a way that he would never love me back? I couldn't sleep, I couldn't eat, I cried often and begged the most high take the torture I was under away. I bled more than I had ever bled before. I thought my previous experiences of miscarriages were bad, this one I will never forget. I felt my soul was ripped from my very being. I feared the bathroom for the loss I would see. When it was seen, well I could only say Jah helped me to witness the loss as I cleaned up the evidence from my body and from the floor. I could hardly cope with all it entailed.

The transition that I had experienced during the past weekend had reminded me of the events of my loss, and had put me in touch with King's loss too. I had the chance to express a lot with King on my third day, so I felt better than I did on "The Second Day" King had spend a good while with me during that evening. I am so very grateful, and give thanks for that. The end of my menstrual transition however was not to be until I had an ultrasound in order to witness an empty uterus. This I did not want to face alone, but what did I do? I did not tell him again. Every time I brought up the subject I sensed the vibes from him. He held either side of his head, he screwed up his face, he sighed and he got defensive. I got defensive too. I couldn't bear for him to say he didn't want to talk about it again, so I held onto the pain again. Oh Jah, the pain is, as you know it to be, so bad, so bad. I told him of my appointment for the morning. I found it hard to even say it for fear of his rejection again. Instead, he was attentive to me and aided me in my speech as to why I needed to have an ultrasound. I felt low as he expressed that he could not be with me for the morning.

The fundamental thing about our reasoning's was that we got on a level that we both had never been on together before, or should I say with another. He knew it to be true as did I, we didn't say things like "Its strange isn't it", that was not important and had no meaning to what we reasoned on. I sometimes made the mistake of not expressing what I should to him. (Conditioning, you see) He was not aware that his mother knew of the situation regarding the pregnancy. Look, even she was unaware at the beginning, but as the weeks went by, she was the one that was there for me when I was bleeding.

My Queen was worried about the length of time I was bleeding and with the amount, so she continued to call in on me due to her concern and of her experience in women's health. She made sure the children did their chores so that I could rest and repair. It was her who I called when I became distressed with my loss of blood although she was unaware of my miscarriage, (Or was she) as she cried with me. My bleeding had become more worrying to her when I began to flood, so she brought me to the hospital. This was a blessing; as I really needed support and she had obviously received my spiritual message. I received a message that morning too. It was a txt from King. He thanked me for my love but showed me that his love belonged to his "Soul mate", he wanted us to be friends and no more.

I felt nothing but extreme pain from the very depths of my being and had to hold onto myself as I fell to the ground. I called on the most high to carry the pain for me and experience my penalty, until I could get up and accept it for what it was. I felt hot, I felt cold, I felt sick and I felt weak but most of all I felt the love that the most high had joined me with, reject me in a way and at a time that made me feel death all around me.

At the hospital, I removed my clothes to reveal my loss as I became as cold as ice in my physical and emotional pain. My Queen was very upset at what she had seen and she cried. I could smell that sweet smell of my mother which brought me back to the peace that awoke me "Mother, are you there"? I said as I still fought to hold back the last remnants of the pregnancy "Yes, I am here" my Queen said. I held on to her and I cried like a baby. I told Queen that I had lost my King, and that I had lost myself. She did not make the connection as I had told her I had not been intimate with King. She held onto me and said nothing. I hated that lie. I told her a week later (still bleeding), that I had lost her son's baby. She was upset with both King and me for not being careful, but she was not surprised, as she knew how much I loved him. She also thought he loved me. She did however tell

98

me not to tell King about the pregnancy. That hurt me even more, as I had so much pain to bear already, I was not sure if I could hold back for much longer or even if she had the right to ask me to. I didn't hold it for long as (Yes you guessed), why should I not tell him? So I did.

The transition at hand was still imminent during this time with King as was my need to express. We decided that I would read a song he had written to aid the transition.
Reading his songs as I said "Sent me alone in a golden cave" The words always totally related to me at that moment or trauma that I had faced recently. He was always aware of when I became open, so he gave me one of the songs he had recently written. Well, it hit me hard. So hard, that my being and I could not hold back the feelings that I had about what I had held from him because of protecting him from pain. (We women must stop doing that). The tears just appeared. I felt an empty space inside me that could not be filled, not even by him anymore.

I had not let myself be cared for and still did not succeed in protecting him. I know he feels pain and I feel it every time we talk about it. We both feel pain, but are working at it, really we are. We are still there for each other and ourselves. It just hurts that's all. I cried. I cried a lot a whole lot before I could part from him. I could barely stop myself, so I cried a little longer. I felt warm in his arms, I felt safe. There was no longer a reason to hold back from what I was feeling. I missed him and had to tell him. The most high aided me through, as I felt myself saying, "I love you, I love you, oh King, King, it hurts so bad, my god, my god, please Jah, Jah help me". I could feel the spider was beginning to devour me and my soul was withering away. I just had to call for help. I called Jah and he came to my rescue and he saved me. I needed to cry and I needed King at that time, to hold me, like he never held me before, because I needed him to tell me oh Jah, to tell me that he loved me too just then, even though he wouldn't.

Over the weeks I had retreated to a "Safe zone" in order to protect myself from further pain, only to find that I was merely destroying myself. Somehow I still feel it happening as in my efforts to be open and true by allowing myself to love him with my heart and soul I still lose. Why is this so I ask myself? Well, I suddenly realised that denying that this love was happening to me, had not helped me to grow as free as I want to grow, so I need to continue to feel and express the love that I have to give openly and be open to what I may or may not receive in return.

Thank you Jah for being there to guide me through this time.

Rastafari Spiritual Powers dwell within my very soul.

Enough said

Queen Irena.

21. LOVE IS A SPIDER'S WEB
Emails to a Queen
Strings Of The Heart

Greetings Queen Imani.

It has been a while, I know. The transitions within my life take many turns, as it is so for the web of the Most High spider.

I have been inspired to write again but there is so much to say about my love, passions, hurts, wants, needs, desires, rejections, acceptance and ambitions. Many days have gone, yet to be depicted. I can only begin right here right now with what I am feeling. I give the very most thanks to the very Most highest being within my soul and everlasting spirit that Jah is with my life and my love for all eternity. I feel the spirit hold me when I talk, more and more each day. I feel I am being prepared to meet spirit to spirit and there is no turning back from the Most High, as he tugs away at me while I remain stuck within this web.

I had the opportunity to reason with the Most High through his spirit within his son (King) a few moments ago. Its funny, I have to laugh. I laughed all the way home from his yard. I just couldn't stop. I laughed because of all the pain that we had both gone through over the past week. Yes, over the pain. It seems that no matter how hard that all was, we reasoned, smiled at each other, held hands and laughed. I read about his pain in his songs (they were very deep and written with all the feelings that he had experienced), it showed me only what I already knew, but that was all right. That was not difficult, In fact I had a great time. If I am not mistaken, we laughed at ourselves for the madness regarding everything between us and at the deep love we still committed to one another along with both families. . We will always have time for each other. The vibes are spiritual and create a sweet peace bond between us. Let me tell you the best way I can about this transition on the subject of my sweet King. First of all, he will always be my sweet King because he is. That sweetness only I can see it that way. Secondly, He holds me when I cry, he sits in silence with me, he smiles with me in acknowledgement of the stress we both face in our lives and he attend to my needs on my 'Red days'. He laughs at my sexual encounters, supports and enhances my actions, he feeds and cares for my children, he encourages my sisters, loves my Queens and he respects my Kings.

Anyway, I went away for the weekend (yes, alone as usual), I went to a caravan. It was great as I took all my most important music, food, candles, incense, clothes, writings and scriptures, not to mention my weed. I danced and sang at the top of my voice with the music blaring. I swam and floated until I was told not to as, well, I looked dead. I could overs their concern. Queen, I am very much alive and will be for a long time to come. I spent quality time with the Most High, and was shown what was to come and what is to be.

I was able to feel and express what I needed to at that time, give thanks for my two eldest children. I have been blessed with their over standing of my needs as their appointed mother, for them being able to organise and run the family in my absence. Jah will remain their birth mother and father even when I become too tired to continue.

At the beginning of the week there was another plan for this weekend, King and I were to go away. As the time drew nearer the spirit of the most high showed us both that the plan needed to be changed as although this may have seemed a good idea at the time, our love for each other became too complicated to continue on this path. This might seem strange, but believe me Queen; I felt it and knew before it came to the surface. We had both become defensive and tearful. The lack of sleep seemed to be mutual and food had no taste. Due to my care for my children, I had not made these feelings a priority until we had our time together.

We went out to lunch, that felt good but a little artificial as we could talk any way, but the talking was usually within the borders of our stressful lives. We felt we needed to break a little ice before we were meant to go away together. I felt his pain and my soul had read the spirits right. It was only a matter of time now. To inspire this event, I wrote to him so he would know beforehand what was happening to me and what I was feeling. I know he probably had prepared all kind of things to say to me but this time he needed guidance as most men do (We even aid them in the breaking of our hearts, because we know when it's coming. Man, we're good). This is what I know I had to do for him. Thursday was a very difficult morning, afternoon, evening, night, midnight and so on. I cried, and cried. Father knows how I held onto my breasts and my soul, and cried for his love. I think you know what I mean.

Sunday night while I was away, I cried too. Don't get me wrong Queen, I am in no way distraught as I still know who I am, I love life, my family and most of all the Most High. That will always be. The tears that I cried were all about losing a part of the best and most precious love from a King that I would have ever held. I know that, this kind of love will only ever come to me and be shown to me once in a lifetime. I cannot imagine this love again with another. After all, this was my friend. There was never an announcement that we were in a relationship that a one would clearly recognise, we just happened.

My dear Queen, those same feelings put me in a complete hold, when King showed me how he felt about Jane. It was so deep; I felt my heartbeats slowed down. I thought and prayed that she felt this way about him and that she tells him these things. At that moment I found it hard to breathe. I suppose I need to explain to you that every single word that he had just said to me regarding the feelings he had for her, were the same feelings that I had always had for him. The smells, the shaking, the glow, the warmth, and the peace everything, and it shook me, it shook me badly. The phones cut off, as it was doing throughout our reasoning but now just in time for me to be sick, drink water build a very strong Splif and pray to the Most High for the strength to call him back. I prepared myself to rise while Jah took control of my being. My mind opened over the words he had expressed to me, and I struggled to show him that I would never stop loving and feeling the deepest love for him.

My heart had actually slowed and my being had changed drastically in order for me to talk with clarity. I was able to show King that he must be with the woman he felt these feelings for. I am truly happy that he felt able to say what he did. I know it was hard for him, but girl, only the highest power could have aided me through that night in place of the death of my soul. It was hard for me too, in many ways. It left me in total wonder as to why she was not breaking her legs to be with this sweet King through thick and thin. Why had he turned to me when it should had been her? Why was she not there for him? Why must he wait for her when she clearly knows how he feels and what he needs? Had I filled the space that she could not? Where is her spirit, Jah? Where is she? Why is he in so much pain when their love is to be? Shouldn't it be just plain and simple? What did I fill for him? What does he want from me? Is he afraid to ask? Is he afraid to let go of me? Is he afraid to let go of her? (Dare I say it in case its true) What need do I fill for him? Is it because no matter what she feels for him, he feels this way so it has to be? What need did I fill for him? Where is her love for him? Does she not show him? Is that why he turned to me? Is it because of my love? Why do I still need his love? Why does he need mine? What need do I fill for him then? Do I want him to be wrong? Is he sure he is doing the right thing? Am I?

Some time ago I showed King that the lyrics to a precious song I listen to, expressed the ultimate love of a woman. I listen to it often and feel it to the bone. I don't know if he has even overed what that meant, or if he even listened to it as deep as he should. Its not that I feel he has to prove anything to me regarding her love, as the proof is already apparent, she is not here, its just that, why did he turn to me? Was there or is there something missing that I fill. I guess there is. Is he afraid to say? Why?

Returning home from my time away had its tearful moments too regarding my thoughts on the depths of my loneliness amongst the busy life that I lead, but as the Most High moves within me, so too does my willingness to move forward into the realities of my life and those that want and need my complete love. This will always belong and be for my precious children. They provide for me the will to be free to love them with all that I am, and hold. At the times I feel totally isolating while they spin with me in this world. Although this is a heavy load, I wouldn't want it any other way. I am completely myself within the midst of my life and my love. The Most High had given my children to me because I asked him to. As for the experiences of the love that we share, well there is no higher level, as it is of the Most High power. The love between mother and child will be eternally right here within me. The love I shared with my mother? Oh Jah, can anyone ever overs that. She is the reason that I am.

I give thanks oh gracious mighty one for my Highest Queen Mother. Through "Livity", she moves with the father.

Selah.
Your Queen Irena.

22. LOVE IS A SPIDER'S WEB
Emails to a Queen
Queens.
How Much Do I Love Thee

Queen Imani

How are you my sweet angel? I just want to express to you how precious you are to me. In fact, I want to express my feelings to you as my Queen and dedicate this chapter to all the Queens in my life and my love. How precious you all are. You know whom I write of, from the time you even start to read what I am about to say, as your heartbeats become the drums in the night.

My Queens, my dear Queens, how much do I love thee? I hope you don't think that the love we have for our men and children can ever come in the way of you and me, and the love that we share. No way. Without us there could not even be them, so lets set the record straight right here and right now. For the men in our lives there is at times only fear of our love. They show this when they try to curfew us, or criticise us, or blame us for their love of us. They want to hide us and keep us away from each other, because they are afraid to be real and love as deep as us. As for our children, well if we did not have this connection, our children would not have so much pleasure with us and be able to express that to us and feel that from us. When we show our love, they are there to witness and to be guided towards a special bonding that only a woman can have with her children. Without our shared love, they would be lost. Without our love, we would not find peace and therefore become free to give them the love that they desire and need so much from us. For as much as you all know what is in my heart, this energy needs to be expressed to you, just for you, my Queens.

I love you, I admire you, I feel you, I want you, I need you, I recognise you, I adore you, I visualise you, I respect you. I create with you; I feel pain for you and with you. I empathise with you and I get vexed with you, but I won't argue with you, because I worship you. My Queens.

I can touch you, I can caress you, I can kiss you, I can squeeze you, and I can please you. I can look on you and tell you that you are so sexy, got lovely breasts, a wicked ass and hold them. I can stroke your hair and tell you I love you. We can hold hands in the street without a care because we know true love, don't we, my Queens? We are truly blessed to be what we are and where we are, floating with royalty, covered with royalty, talking of royalty, feeling with royalty, because we are nothing less then Queens.

I met a long time friend who I hadn't seen for around thirteen years apart from for a brief moment about five years back. Helen was sitting in traffic going one way, while I was moving gradually the other way. Our eyes met, and Queens, my heart began to beat so fast and my breasts began to burn. There she was, with her glowing face and diamond eyes, her hair was as black as the night, glittering with the stars. Her royalty was showing. What a wonderful and beautiful sight and being she is. Her beauty beheld me and I shouted out "Helen, my sweet darling Queen, my baby". She reached her hand out to me and her eyes began to shine so very brightly.

There was a single tear rolling down one cheek and a pool of tears ready to depart from the eye above the other cheek. I reached out to her but our hands did not meet, so I pulled mine back, put it to my lips and sent to her the very essence of my soul, within my kiss. She licked her lips in acceptance, looked at me and said "Don't worry, we will meet up again soon".

I looked in front of me to see that my traffic had long gone, only her traffic and what was behind me had remained on the road. I told her that I loved her and she responded with her love of me back. She bit her bottom lip and closed her eyes in passion. I drove off holding my breast, and feeling that I had seen deep within her, and had recognised the royal threshold that she was on. I did not want to leave her, (my heart still beating fast), and she certainly did not welcome our parting, but we both had faith that we would connect again some fine day to take another flight together.

Queens, these feelings are not just a one off for me, this love that I feel is real, deep, sensual, overwhelming, passionate and exciting. It just takes my breath away.
When I am with my Queens, nothing comes between what I feel for them and nothing ever will. When I say with them, I do not just talk of the physical power. The spirits that move within us reach out and call. They call at any time or anywhere. We always bow to each other and feel the connections. The power of the Most High holds us and sometimes we just have to laugh out loud in recognition when we look into each other's eyes, but we also fall into each other's arms and into each other's souls.

When I saw my queen Helen, my children were with me. They did not object to the holding up of traffic, because they knew they were safe and also knew that nothing must come between the love I have for my Queens. They see and over stand the power and feel it too and it pleases them. (I Give thanks)

I know for some, reading the above was a little heavy, and particularly out of the ordinary, but there are many who care to reason on this matter, that feel the same vibrations too. Only those who have seen it and felt it will ever over stand it. This too, is within the care of the I and on the Most Highest level. You do not have to be rich nor covered in particular garments, as the power of his spirit within our souls is there especially if you have nothing. It can only be reached if you know and believe and have faith in the fact, that what you hold in your depths is pure and true. Behind it all of course, is the Most High power to guide us through the valleys of peer pressure, ego, stereotypes, embarrassments, family ethics, and jealousy in order to get us to the Promised Land, where milk and honey flow through our veins in order to prepare us for the heights of Zion and the inevitable spectacular royal climax.

May our spirits continually connect with our souls and lift us to everlasting heights and coat our nakedness in the purest of liquid gold, that flows from the Mountains of Zion onto the tops of our heads, continuing around and into the very depths of our being. I pray that when we swing our arms in flight over and above the world, that we continually shower the chosen with essences from our souls and show them, our way home.
Selah.
Queen.Irena
LOVE

23. LOVE IS A SPIDER'S WEB
Emails to a Queen
Yes The Thongs Are On

Greetings to you Queen.

Guess what! I awoke in a laugh of erotica this morning. Please get ready to rise because you are about to fly with me.

I had a dream about the fulfilment of my passions. First of all it has to be said that in order to fly, you have to be on the right plane. The kind of plane that would take you into a place where the Queens are. Feel the power, feel the vibrations, see their colours, see their eyes. Welcoming glares and magical touches. We are holding and stroking each other with passion and pleasure. We reason on how to get pleasure from our men. It is deep and sensual. A Queen raises up to display how she wants to be taken and where she wants to be touched. Another Queen shows her over standing of what she had seen. Other Queens show them what to wear and more about how to touch themselves. It gets hot, very hot. The heat is to do with the laughing about the taking up of room, as we take our places within the room. Garments are displayed on our bodies. Yes, the thongs are on, old bras off and new holsters on. What a lift. I didn't know my breasts could look like that, I feel so sensual.

I transform into my totally sexual state and think and feel all that I desire. (I wonder if you really want me to go on, or should I stop right here) All right, you asked for it. I lie back and (No, not think of duty, that is for them and this is all for me). I am touched. I am stroked and kissed by a thousand lips from the top of my head, my eyes my ears, neck, my chin, nose, shoulders and oh my god, I have to stop, too much pleasure. I try to get away but cannot, it's too late. I am screaming because my breasts were about to explode with the amount of sucking and squeezing that they are going through, not to mention the passion that I am experiencing. I spin with the pleasure of it all. It seems to go on forever. "Can I handle what is imminent?", I ask myself. I have to because I want it so very much. While I fly, the weight of the passion brings me back to my bed for the ecstasy I am to go through.

Screaming with the pleasure of the passion I feel, I shout "Stop, Jah help me". A voice came to me that said, "This is my gift to you, I will pour my pleasure onto you and you will receive me". I give in and stop struggling like a button had just been pressed. All hell breaks loose (As the saying goes) my stomach, my navel, "Oh my god, I want you, just take me, please take me". I am rolled over and am passionately kissed and sucked while I am lying there laughing and screaming. I am rolled back and I am sucked in my most sacred of places. Queen, this of course sets my soul on fire and I could barely move. My head is the only part of my body that is free, so I toss it to and fro trying to break free form this extreme feeling. My breasts are still on fire, as they are not left alone. I pray this will never end as I shake with the almighty power that controls me. "You belong to me", I scream out, and ,oh my god, and there is more to come.

My body begins to shake with a stronger power and "Jah, is that you"? I see a bright light in the depths of my being and he is inside me, suddenly I am set free and we climb frantically while we give each other the sweetest of passion. (Yes, passion is the right word because that is what I want now). I scream in orgasm as it lasts forever. I can hardly breathe and my heart is pounding like a drum it is so intense. I reach the light and I become transparent. Then I am transformed back into a visible being that is witnessed by all around me. "Look at Queen, she knows" I hear them say. I look up and smile as I open my eyes to look at their glory as it all happens to me.

I am taken back to where I was and I am set upon again, this time my breasts are left for last. I am kissed and sucked everywhere over and over again slowly and I am groaning with delight. My pubic areas are engulfed with desire and I cry with intense laughter. It is so delightful to feel the warmth, the want, the need and the passion of love and to receive it. They hold me firmly while they kiss me. They hold me firmly while they suck me gently. They climb onto me as they, oh no, not my breasts; they are still on fire, (which is why they are left till last). My nipples are enormous by now but are engulfed by the juiciest of lips that suck and lick them to death. It sets my soul on fire too and my body begins to dance. I hold heads as I rise and my mouth opens wantonly as I reach other heights. I am floating with them and I am open to any and everything.

I come back down and we climb and hold on, while sucking and biting with passion. There is so much juice and it tastes delicious. I have never seen nor felt so much passion and I love it. While I experience my orgasms, I am carried and paraded into a large crowd. My body is dancing and I do not object to the crowd, neither to the orgasms. I groan and groan and feed myself by licking the juices off from my fingers, having collected it from my body. I lick my lips, part my legs and I am taken again and again, each time I am the main focus and it is all for me as I was told.

The last orgasm is different. I have risen to take over. I want to give passion, but there are so many to choose from. I choose two of them and start, with throwing cold water on them to cool them down. I don't wait for them to complain about the shock of it so I position them, one kneeling in front and one kneeling behind and me. I am between them. They want to touch but I won't let them (not yet anyway), not until I dance my body while I brush past them. Their bodies swell and they hold their heads with the pressure. One of them make attempts to holds me down. This is against the rules, so he is taken away, for a while against his will, by those who protect me. I lie on my back, and use both hands to guide the remaining manhood around my lips licking occasionally. Of course this is too much for him to bear, so he grabs hold of my head and thrusts his well-developed self into my mouth. He is definitely out. I push him away and he is held to watch. I show my ready lips to the one I rejected first, and he is set free.

He has never been so ready, so I lick him with delight. When he reaches his time, he screams but I would not let him hold me, he is held by others who let him go when I indicated to them. He is so grateful, as by now he is begging for mercy. When liberated, he releases over me in time for me to continue dancing whilst I rub his juices over my neck, my breasts, my stomach, but mostly over my sacred place. I prolong this touch in order to ready myself for more. You may be wondering what happened to the one rejected. Well, don't, as I call him forward to fuck me, and he obliges, so I fuck him right back. I awoke.

I remembered where the dream had started and was very grateful to my Queens who had guided me and were with me throughout my pleasures and were lifted by what they had seen. I was not afraid and had given what I wanted and had received what I needed, love, passion, lust and desire.

I am certainly going through this transition with some scary, exciting and powerful experiences. I just can't stop laughing and smiling too. The one feeling that remains with me right now is that The Most High truly loves me and I am truly feeling it too. I am eternally thankful for the lessons and for the pleasures of my dreams.

Queen.

24. LOVE IS A SPIDER'S WEB

Emails to a Queen

Wishful Thinking

Queen Imani

I pray you managed to get over the last part, as you need strength to deal with this next excerpt. Yes, here we go again. I seem to be going through this erotic transition stage so I might as well wallow in it all. I had another dream again but this time the main characters were my one and only King and I.

Had a heavy session in the gym and went off to shower. It was late and I was last to prepare to go home. King was fixing up to leave while waiting for me. I was attempting to hurry, as he wanted to get away from the building as soon as he could.

The water was very refreshing so without realising, I stayed a little longer then I thought. With my eyes closed, taking in the temperature of the water splashing on me, I was unaware of him calling me from outside. Suddenly he made his naked presence known to me. (No, he did not call me when he came into the shower area), I felt his lips on my neck. He was sucking it. "Hey", I cried out as I turned around, "What the hell are you doing in here"? I felt a deep flow running through my body (I think this was my blood rushing around, it must have been, as my heart was pumping fast). He laughed and said, "What do you think I am doing here, we're alone aren't we? I told you that you have no idea how far I would go". He pulls me back towards him, holds onto my roots and pulls my head back to ravish my neck. I say nothing but grab his waist and thrust him closer. I want him so badly by now, that I don't care what he wants to do with me because I was absolutely dying for it.

I push him away and start to run out of the shower area laughing. He is surprised by this and shouts after me "Come back, I have something for you, you know, Queen." He rushes after me and catches hold of me. We are in fits of laughter and fall to the ground. He drags me towards him and begins to bite my feet, calves, and thighs. I am laughing and kicking, but scream out "Stop, you're going to make me explode, stop, stop. Then, no don't, If you stop, I am going to kill you". I give in and lie there with my eyes waiting and wanting while panting with passion for what he was about to do, and he does it. He bites into me, and then sucks me hard.

I am sure you know by now if that does anything for me at all. Queen, fire is in my soul. I hold his head and look down to witness him taking me to pieces, as my desire for more becomes a must. I cannot move further as he takes hold of my hands, in order to stop my disturbing of his contribution towards the quenching of this thirst for passion that we both have. I am screaming for mercy, as it is much too much for me to hold back on the noise. This is my King that is devouring me; I think, as I continually shake and pant. It feels so intense as I scream; he has me in such a hold. I am about to reach the ceiling with his actions and see there is a light, I see his face through this in front of mine and ah, thank god he enters me with a thrust. I cry out with the sweet pain that I feel within me as it all happens. I cannot begin to describe this sensation in simple terms.

We are kissing frantically and sucking lips, and necks as he travels down to my breasts and bites deeply into either side of them in turn. The pain is shocking now and I am griping him with ecstasy as we dance vigorously while he penetrates me over and over again. We are both panting, and gasping for breath, we cannot laugh, as it is getting hot and extremely obsessive now. We reach the highest of heights. I don't want this to end and tell him "Don't stop, please don't stop". He is very responsive to this plea and thrusts himself deeper and deeper inside me, lifting my legs then holding them apart for a deeper impact. My head lifts up and drops back down. I can't stand it; my mind is screaming. Am I really dreaming? "Sweet Jah, I want you." I reach the heavens ultimate limits, and he is right there with me as we rise high with this ecstasy. We scream and scream with this power and fall over each other into a heap on the floor with water continually pouring on us from the showers.

He gets up and leads me into the changing rooms. I stand there watching him in astonishment over what had just happened. "Queen" he says, "This is no dream, this is real, are you ready for me"? I take my chances and tell him "I want you to ignite me". He is rubbing my breasts and I am holding his erection. We laugh while grabbing at each other as we begin again right there in the changing rooms. He slams me against the lockers, devours my lips while I devour his. I go down and lick his manhood. Forget Ice poles on a hot summer's day; this is where it's at.

He bangs on the lockers because of his ecstasy and is about to explode, but I stop. He is shocked and is in pain, screaming, wanting to release. Of course I told him to ignite me, but he just has to catch me first. I run back toward the showers. You better believe, he is there before me, and to pull me down onto him I accept him with the greatest of pleasure. "No, no, oh my god. No, he screams and explodes into a rage of desire as I suck his nipples and bite his breasts. He releases deep inside me as it lasts eternally, like a fountain pouring its contents out. Still screaming, he holds onto his manhood while I remove myself from him. He had not finished releasing, so he pulls me back onto him and pumps every last drop into me. I am totally filled with what he has offered me, and fall backwards followed by him with his tight hold on me, and we take flight. We roll holding on together until we stop, to lie there with the refreshing water still flowing. We can barely laugh at the excitement and raunchiness of it all so we just look on each other and smile broadly (still panting). What a stimulating powerful experience. It felt extremely spiritual, sensual and exciting. I awoke.

My dream rocked my soul when I awoke, as I could smell his aroma on me and taste him on my tongue. I realised that the sensations I now felt, showed me that I had released my very core in this dream as I swam within his aroma. Queen, I know you overs what that whole experience has done for me.

Yours

Queen.Irena

25.LOVE IS A SPIDER'S WEB
Emails to a Queen
My Reality Is

Dearest Imani.

I greet you with an explanation of the recent feelings that I had shown to you within my writings and pray that it can shed light on what is going on for me within this almighty web.

I suppose I am feeling a little subdued regarding my sexuality. I have become aware that my desires have been on hold for some time now. With my experiences of disrespect, loneliness, ugliness, deception and rejection, I had forgotten what it was like to receive the passion that I had always been willing and able to give without thinking. I had become sexless. I can almost say lifeless, as I remember expressing my need for love and passion to Omar even when I loved him deeply. This merely aided his need in his rejection of me. In fact it had been so throughout my life.

Since I had become free and more open to my feelings, I grew to be aware that my sensual side was resurfacing, so I just went with the flow. I began to wear my royal garments more often and decorated my body and hair again like I used to. I say used to, as before this I had become closed and did not want anyone to see my glory because I certainly did not feel that way without receiving the love that I so needed. Now of course, I am looking after my body and my soul is being fed with the most wonderful and uplifting experiences, therefore sooner or later my sexual desires were bound to erupt.

I have to admit; I feel so lustful right now that it is making me mad with a want for an almighty passionate encounter. I want any part of my dreams to be real. Well, maybe not the crowd, but all the rest. It is so hard not to think about what happened in those dreams. I even feel a little embarrassed for myself as my soul grieves. No, don't be worried for me; it is just that, to be open in that way about my sexuality, well I may have pushed him further away from me. You know who I mean as he has been there from the start and I had not shown him this part of me until now. (Although it has not diminished since I have known him) Yes, Queen. Not only has he read about the dreams, I read them to him too. I was so very nervous and felt threatened by it. It is nothing that he said or did (Or was it), I suppose it is to do with the love between us (or is it the love that I feel)

You see Queen, lust and passion is somewhat different to desire for me, as with lust and passion, it allows those involved to laugh while indulging with me without the emotional attachments of desire. Sometimes my desired love gets in the way of having great fun. This is where my embarrassment, nervousness and a little sadness come in.

One of my first approaches towards King was to ask him if he wanted to have some sexual lust (although I always knew our relationship would be special and unique without that), he had not to this day answered that question. Instead, we just continued to grow towards one another while we shared our desires, so we fell into a love that changed our lives. At the same time, I continued to sort for the quenching of my desires through lust and was able to get that and it was great fun. That situation had dwindled for me, because I had become so filled with love for King, that I had forgotten my desires again until the dreams came. Queen; don't think that I have not felt sexual during this time, as you would be so wrong. I just had not been able to quench that burning fire with anyone. I feel lust and passion all the time now, as it seems much easier to handle then the love, desire and rejection. I say the word rejection a lot, don't I. Well that feeling has stayed with me for many reasons, and for a long time, and it is affecting me badly enough to screw it all away.

Heavy stuff you might think, but Queen, I have felt this way for too long. No, its not just because of him, I need to feel unconditional pleasure, real love because I know I truly deserve it now, but where the hell from. I find myself getting so pissed off with all the demands of life and have to lock myself in my room at times and cry in peace. (No, I do not wish my family away or to be different), but lord have mercy, what about what I want and what I need. I feel I will explode with what I desire.

I told King that I might need to stay away from him for a little while because of my desires and my dreams. He actually asked me if I could control it. I told him I did not want to. (I really don't think I should) Although I was able to write about the dream I had about the two of us on this occasion, I have had the same dream over and over again. So no, I do not want to control it, as I am already controlling the love feelings because of all the pain that it had caused. (I don't mean our friendship love, as that is safe) If he is concerned about me making advances to him outside our special friendship hugs, then he needs to tell me that. He says he will control himself, from what? I don't suppose he would tell me that and I don't suppose he would tell me if he wants a good fuck with me either, as that is what he is like. In fact, I am beginning to think that he will remain sexless and refuse to indulge himself in passion or allow himself to have any fun, until his soul mate is finally ready for him even if it takes another eleven years from now. He stops himself from becoming sexual even though he is extremely sensual and sexy. He even stops himself from dreaming about being sexual. He has become closed like I was. Why the hell does he need to do that to himself?

Anyway, I am making stronger attempts to open up to others, so I will make sure I go out there, with or without company, with the aim to receive love. This may take some time but Queen I am certainly going to make that effort. No I am not going to deal with just anyone, as I know that I deserve quality. I know, (as we all do) that in my attempts to find a one that I can connect with, have a laugh with and deal with the passion whenever I need it, I may feel degraded by the quality that I find so I might have to make my mind stone-like in order to release what I need to. This (as we all know) is about making choices. I also think of the barriers my children would put up against anyone that I happened to want as my life partner after their father. So don't be surprised if I crawl into my safe zone again for protection, because the powers of the Most High is always right there for me, especially in my dreams.

I send to you and your royal family my strongest blessings. May Jah keep you safe in this time. Selah

Queen Irena

26. LOVE IS A SPIDER'S WEB
Emails to a Queen
What Is Your Status

Queen. Greetings

I have realised something. The Kings that are unattached, (or seem to be) are in pain, in so much pain over ended relationships that they find it difficult to relate to a Queen in the way they need to in order to repair themselves. Yes, they need us so badly that they don't even realise it.

I suppose I must explain myself here I know. We as Queens tend to be direct in our attention (and rightly so) to men that show themselves to us, we catch on though (when we become intimate with them) as all they want to do is cry out their hearts to us because they feel safe with us when we comfort them. What pain they carry. Oh Jah I feel it for them at times.

I was able to quench my thirst for passion last night with a friend. I first (having prepared myself for the event) needed to assist him to relax in order for him to feel free to feel with me. He was so tense. We reasoned on the issues of letting go and were able to begin to make love. Yes, we made love. I suppose we both needed tenderness first in order to receive what we were both lacking at that time, and it was good, Queen. It helped us both. We didn't reach our heights, as we needed to stop so he could cry a little, but that was all right with me, as I know he was feeling emotional pain so I asked if he wanted us to stop. He did not want to as he had recovered. We rolled over and had the heated sex we also both needed, and that I can say was good because the stars were with me as they always are during this time. As for him, well, he was in a state, of course, and cried again while telling me that he was not ready for us to go further than friends, he also said he didn't want to lose me because we had been intimate, as he needs me in his life. "I respect you and I respect your family so much, Queen Irena," he said. Surprise!

Its not that I was looking for more, (well not from him) as I had become sensitive to the fact that he was vulnerable, I have just heard this so many times it is like a broken record being played. It's just that sometimes a Queen needs a one to be strong for her because we need to be strong all the time for ourselves, our children, and our men. I need a one who is strong. I know he will find it difficult to visit me for a while, but I also know that (Being the Queen I am), sooner or later I will stop by his place to say it is ok, and he will feel free again, by the royal care that I always have to give.

Why are our men in so much pain? First of all, I say "Our men" because they are. They all belong to us. We give birth to them, we grow them, we nurse, we teach them and show them the Most High, we give them every part of our love and have their best interest at heart, but yet they are still in pain. Why don't they want to listen to us and be the Kings they are supposed to be? Is it because of the women that hurt them? Why do they hurt them any way? We can only know for ourselves who we are and what we give them.

As a Queen amongst so many others, I know that there are catalogues of women that are so very hurt too, by so many men. Notice that I did not use a royal status just then. That is because that kind of pain does not belong amongst us. I did not say we don't experience it, as we all have the longest and most painful stories to tell. In fact this book could be full of them, but this book is not about that. What I express through my life in the spider's web is my experiences through the love that I feel and express to those around me that I am intimate with. Having said this, I have in no way discarded the fact that the amount of pain felt by those I relate to have relevance in my life, because it does, as every emotion felt has its purpose even for me.

The royal status is clear to me though when it comes to the Queens, but I think you must wonder at times, where my mention of Kings will fit in. Well my Queen, I am at the moment finding it hard to come across a man that has recognised his royal status, there are so many of them. Why can they not see that? When we mention it, they get defensive and blame us for their realisation of our status. The fact that the Queens meet and are lifted by each other has become such a threat to them. It is frightening to be aware of the lengths they would go to keep us apart, or to purposely destroy a queen that obviously expresses her deepest love for her King. Jah have mercy!

As for the women that hurt them deliberately, well they are so lost and do not respect themselves. These women have no over standing of the war they have began. No, I have not forgotten the pain that has been caused by countless men, as I have spent a lifetime carrying that pain within my soul, along with aiding the assisting of countless women in the discovery of their own royalty. I have been right there with them in the valley of eating disorders, searching for the love that we had forgotten to give ourselves, the valley of the doormats, and dirt roads that lead to nowhere, the valley of sexual pleasures for our men in order to keep them sweet. (Well, the bills need to be paid don't they?) I hit you in the right place there; I know it, because its true and you know it. A voice just came to me when I wrote that, "Tell them like it is Queen" it said. No, that life is not for us.

Rise oh you mighty Kings, for you are all that we need to feed us with the pure and true love that is within you, we have to fly with our nations of princes' and princesses and connect spirits that fill our souls and make them complete and free again with Jah.

Sometimes I feel a little sad with the amount of work we all have to. It makes me want to go back to bed and sleep, scream at my children, cry in the bath, sit in silence, argue with the Most High, laugh out loud, sing, dance, clean house, lock my room door, scribble, rock myself, sew my own clothes, write my life story, walk miles, beat a drum, punch, stand up strong, cuss, show love and more. I suppose that is why I am experiencing continued hidden talents that help me to express my feelings. Out of all the pain, I have still managed to rise and give thanks for my life.

I give thanks to the Most High for aiding me through my transitions of spiritual and emotional growth.

The Web continues.

QUEEN

27. LOVE IS A SPIDER'S WEB
Emails to a Queen
Say What You Want King

Greetings, on this bright day.

As you know, I have had various feelings over the last few days. This Spider's web is something else.

I thought of my recent episode, so I visited him. He expressed that He did not want another sexual experience with me because of the respect he had for me. This was fine and still is. He seemed ashamed at what had happened and found it hard to talk with me. I didn't stay long but left without any negative thoughts towards him or over what happened between us. We are adults and both consented to what had taken place.

This morning he arrived in bad spirits; he had obviously had a bad start to the day and had decided to vent his negative vibes towards me. He explained that he had just seen my older son and was asked about the studio. "I am tired of the pressure that I am under from everyone around me". He said. I asked him if I had put pressure on him. "Yes" be butted in. "How" I asked him. He continued, "What even happened with us the other day, you knew I was vulnerable and you knew that I respect you and you came on to me and totally disrespected me, totally." Not surprised by what he had said (are we ever?) I asked him what other pressures are on him, (thinking, "R. C"). He goes on a little about the disrespect that many people around him are showing him, so I butted in and said, "Look, you made it clear to me that your love is your music and that your aim is to get into a studio and do your works. You came to my yard, played me your creation and made more with King and that was good, so what are you saying?" He responded "Yes but the studio, is the last thing on my mind right now and I even feel a pressure with that from King as I have things to do first". (If you ever bring your vibes on the subject of my King into this, I am going to fire you) I thought, but said instead "Look, you made it clear to me how you saw me at first, but I respected myself and you enough to show you that there was more to me then your sexual desires."

He couldn't look at me, but he continued. I come to your home and see your children and they call me Uncle and I respect them for that, but Uncles don't sleep with their mothers, think on that". I had a flash thought of the amount of children that have a variety of Uncles in their lives with the multitude of absent fathers in the world. I also thought of the men that feel women should be seen and not touched by anyone, especially if she has a family to grow. I am certainly not made of stone and will not feel bad for the guilt that he is feeling. I ask him, "When a mother is left to grow her children alone, is she not meant to have sexual desires until they grow up and leave home, while their fathers live life to the full?" (Thinking on the concerns he has over his lost love as a sexual being) "I know she has properly had experiences with men out there. Boy, if it weren't for how I feel towards my mother, I wouldn't even look at a woman" He blurted out. I looked at him thinking, "Don't Queen, he cannot handle it". I allowed him. He babbled on a bit and off he went.

Queen, you see what I mean? If I did allow him to do what ever he wanted to me when he first came round, he would be happy, as I would have confirmed his attitudes towards us. He would not have had the experience of my true love and been shown another way to be around a Queen, but he put me on a pedestal then could not forgive himself for experiencing sexual pleasure with me and now expects me to take this on, and feel bad too. What is their problem? I suppose a one-night stand is all right if you don't have to talk to or see a one again. (Is that a woman thing or is it just men that feel this?) I know that for me, I am not going to just hop in and out of the sack with any one that happens along that takes my fancy, I respect myself more than that. Those fathers do not seem to be aware that while we grow our children alone, we also sacrifice the time out needed to recover from their oppression that has led to our ill health and of course to their own downfall. Come on now!

You see my Queen; one cannot assume that our men are all right, far from it. There is a man shortage out there and many Queens have turned their heads from our men and have gone towards other avenues. They want us to be there for them emotionally and spiritually, however when it comes to the sexual, they want to have the experience and pleasure, but feel guilty and embarrassment over the passion we also give them. They feel they will lose their power (We all know they must have the ultimate power, don't we). I had a bitter taste in my mouth following his visit. In fact it made me feel to spit in the toilet, so I did. I even shed a few tears. Rastafari Lives.
Queen.Irena

28.LOVE IS A SPIDER'S WEB
Emails to a Queen
Mother V Queen

My dear Queen

I feel so low today. This feeling I have is to do with the tiredness inside me. I am heavy with this load Jah. Give me a break please Jah.

I get up in the morning and think of the busy day ahead and someone always happen comes in without a single question relating to how I feel as they see me. (Not that they could anyway), I look and I listen. I have no choice of closing off. No choice but to remind them to say it is a good morning and to give Jah thanks for the chance of yet another day. We exchange greetings and they continue to ask for their school clothes. I remind them of where their clothes, are and tell them to leave me alone. What a thing to say to my babies, my sweet babies. I also tell them however, that they are handsome, pretty, a trouble for the girls, my sweet darling, my kissy, my chucks, my baby and my love. Maybe it's not so bad after all then. I remember that they make me tea and breakfast and even fix up my room with pleasure when I ask them too (That's when they find the hidden goodies, the price to pay). We have wonderful family outings and tickle one another. They laugh, and make up jokes with me, sometimes even cry with me. We sing and dance in our disco sessions, and pray and reason together. I laugh at them when they are loaded, with items of my belongings to bring to my room. (Arron, would simply put on my shoes, and walk casually up the stairs holding my bag on his head). What treasures to behold, and be bestowed on me, oh, my lord. You have also given me everything that I wanted, Jah, I thank you so much for that and for believing in me, Jah. I love you too. With all that I am and all that I could ever possibly be, I love you. You remind me of how to be and how to love.

Queen, I live in constant fear of saying and doing the wrong thing with my children, and I am tired. It is easy to do the wrong thing, but so very hard to do right at times. Without his strength I could not go on. I owe it all to Him. "Be merciful and give I the strength to do it right oh my lord. Teach me to over stand this transition to the fullest". I feel my life slipping away at times and wonder how on this earth they managed with it all. How on this earth did our mothers survive and keep order? The elders' strength is certainly far beyond my elements, so I can only bow down and kiss their feet with the respect that I feel in my soul for them. I cannot imagine doing the same at fifty or fifty-five. How, Jah? How will I get there? Is there a magic prayer just waiting for I to say so I may be restored? "I pray oh Yahweh, Father God, Jehovah, Jah Rastafari, El Shaddai, Allah, My Spiritual Niyahbinghi I, Most High, Selassie I, Buddha, Sweet Jesus. Give I life, please give I life. I pray to the elders' and to the spirits of our ancestors and to the spirits within our communities that over stand this Livity.
I pray to you".

Queen.Irena

Am I to be saved for just the I Jah?
Is it the I?
I n I ask this of the I, because I n I see no one there for I
n I Jah. No one.
Am I n I to pretend forever when the I decide to take I n
I Jah? How long is it to be?
I n I feel so lonely. Will it be forever? Forever is such a
long and dusty road.
I n I feet are hurting as bad as I n I heart is. Hold I n I
Jah, hold I n I in the I light, and rock I n I.
I n I need the I, to hold I n I. I n I feel so lonely with
nowhere to turn.
Is I n I for the I alone?

Help I n I father, come to I n I, walk with I n I, and be
there for I n I.
YOU are I n I Most High.
Come to I n I, and save I n I from this feeling
I n I feel consumed with the grief that I n I sense. Please
do not ask I n I why, as it is too much to bear to the I,
especially as the I overs all.
Just take this time to be silent for I n I, and show I n I,
that the I care for I n I.
Do not be angry with I n I, just be there and show I n I
that, the I care.

Selah

I WONDER WHAT YOU THINK

I wonder what you think; when we share with you king I wonder what you think.
Do you think, "There she goes floating above it all", just because you see we can manage. But this is what we are made of King, what did you think? We stink?

I wonder what you think my dear Queen I wonder what you think.
Did you know we have the overs and only we can create them? You better stop and take a big blink.

Every time we connect, we comfort and love each other, through thin and through thick. How precious we are to one another. Our spirits call on us one-time and we immediately link. We connect at the right time, each point in time. So Praises to the Most High.

Bitter tears we cry. Come let us dry our eyes. Here I wipe your eyes, while you wipe mine. All right now my darling Queen? Have you eaten?
When last did you have a nice dream? Who's doing the children? Do you want me to fix him?
Cos I'm just pissed with him, now Queen (How Dear He Hurt You).
He is just a user, why must you have to be his fool?

We tell each other "No its all right I will manage, it will be ok." Uhmm, "You sure? cos you can sleep here the night, hell you can even stay.

So tempting Queens, so tempting. But do we take up the offer? Well the ones that feel themselves rising will, the others will just go back there and continue to suffer.

I Wonder Who. Was it you?

I wonder who was hurt last night,
I wonder who was held down so tight.
I wonder whose blood ran so bright,
I wonder who was raped last night.

I wonder if she left you mike,
I wonder if he done it by spite.
I wonder if her lights went out,
Don't do it to her man,
Will take years to overs her Plight.

I wonder if she's safe tonight,
From your threats and danger zones John,
I wonder if her bruises show,
I wonder if she's all-alone.

You hurt her bad this time Steve,
You better check she's al right and leave.
What on earth were you thinking just then Ken,
Never fucking do that to a woman again Ben.

You should have washed the dishes instead Nev,
Rather then going off your head Dev.
Now what you gonna do Boo.
Everyone knows it was you.

Not such a charmer after all Saul,
This one's gonna burning a hole Joel.
No more 'Oh isn't he sweet' Pete,
Have to watch where you put your feet, Sweets.

I wonder what it feels like Al,
With no one to turn too now, Sal,

Cant walk and feel safe yourself,
Cos they await you from every shelf.

Should have done better, you might think,
Maybe she'd forgive you, and blame the sink.
Wake up you R***C****,
You can never be sure,
When your pain, will start.

When will it be your turn, Earn?
Are you even slightly concerned? Fire! Burn!
Just wait there a minute, and see, B,
It could be anyone,
Might even be me. SEEN!

29.LOVE IS A SPIDER'S WEB
Emails to a Queen
Preparing To Fly

My Dear Queen Imani

Knowing where to start is at times, a burden, as I have been filled with much inspiration from not only what has gone on in my own story, but also from the lives of those in my love. I say in my love, because they are. My love has included them in my life, in order that the inspirations I receive, can be reasoned with them, my spirits and with the most high that has control of my soul.

My reaction to every action displayed to me by my loves, is what I am learning from. It keeps me in touch with what is real and true in regards to how I feel. Holding my feelings back has never been good for me, as it is so for all of us. At some point or other, actions will always bring them right back to us. How do we respond to them? Do we keep them there inside us forever? Or do we release them? As for me, I have expressed many emotions (well this is what I have allowed you to over stand of me), during the time of my writings.

What has remained constant throughout my transitions is the deepest love that I have with the most high. I reason with the I and all is revealed to me. What to say, what to do and how to be while it happen. I do not always keep to what I had promised the I and pay the price too. At times I have surprised myself, by the level of heights that I have been taken to, as it is so mighty. I even have the cheek to say "Why me" well why not me, has the I not shown I n I that the I is with I n I? You better believe it is clear to I n I.

All the pain and hurt feelings within me were there before I could recognise it, yes sometimes knowledge is also a burden to us, as instead of using this knowledge as a guide for how to move forward and how not to be, we at times get stuck on "Why me". So much pain because of two little words. (Who started that expression anyway)? It cannot be one of us (Or can it)

Every thing I pray for is given to me. It always has been. I say this because most of us pray deepest at a time in our lives, when all hell has turned over for us. (Now let us be honest) the only problem with that is, we do not notice the answers that come during those time and end up saying things like "I pray and pray and I see nothing" or "There is no God." Never mind, let us forgive ourselves right now and start a new if that is so, as there is no forgiveness of you if you cannot forgive yourself first.

I have prayed and searched for love for as long as I could remember, thinking that I had found it on occasions, only to find out otherwise. I have wasted tears and years, but I wouldn't have it any other way because I would not be right here to express this to you. I have all the love that I need right now to be and feel free.

I had been waiting for a chance to write all day, with inspirations flying above me so I could reach up and place it within my writings. I got a message to call my sweet love King, to reason with him. He expressed to me that even if we have perfect love, we will always search for more. He put me in touch with the royal seal of approval that we all seem to be searching for all the time. I think we all know by now that it is not something that is a visible being or we would have found it by now. Some American (Yes American, never African) scientist would have pulled it up from a bottomless pit named something like "Hell raiser". No, only we can find the perfection we search for, but most of us have forgotten to look in the mirror to witness the vessel that will lead us there. There are many who hold on to their perfection, as they believe it is too much to reveal. They choose to be a "Martyr of pain", and take a troubled soul to the grave; do they really feel they deserve that plight?

Throughout the times of my writings, I have been in love. (Yes, I am releasing again so be prepared). I had prayed for a one for me to express my true love with. Funny, I did not have a flash of the children's fathers' but I just forced myself to think of them and lord god, I can't even remember his smile. That says a lot and I thank you, Jah. No, this love is of another. You know whom I talk of, don't you and he does too. I can feel him as I even write and he feels me when he reads what I have to say of him. My love for him was inspired by the answer to my prayer to the Most High, so I do not hide it from here. My love for him is real and royal. My love for him is exceptional. My love for him inspires me to write, laugh, smile, sing, dance, dream, feel passion, feel warm, feel extra sexy during my special times and makes me reason with my Queens on our
Meanings of love.

His love for me, gives me hope and faith in the foundation of men. His love for me, aids me in the respect I have for myself. His love for me, keeps me royal. His love for me makes me weak, makes my heart beat fast and slow. His love for me extends my soul and guides me. His ultimate love for me makes me give him my ultimate love; his love for me invites and excites me, it lowers me and if lifts me.

What kind of love is that? Thank you Jah for that kind of love and for answering my prayer.
Queen.

30.LOVE IS A SPIDER'S WEB
Emails to a Queen
Bondage Of Love

Greetings Queen Imani.

Each day I become more aware that in order to be free, one has to learn to release a great deal of emotion that had been stored away like priceless bottles of wine in a dusty cellar.

Although it would be most interesting and inspirational to take you through them, step by step, that would not be completely possible as it would take forever and a day to both write it and to over come the effect it would have on my soul. I will, however, take you through the transitions uppermost in my life right now as best I can. It would bring comfort to me now and also throw light on the reasoning behind my emotional condition at present.

I spent a long while with my sweet king last night. This was important as he was considering making a call to his doctor regarding mum's medical condition, as it had deteriorated. He had asked me to be with him when he did this. This was to do with the rejection he would face from mum if he followed his thoughts. He needed my support with his actions. I agreed to this as I had concerns about mum, and wanted something to be done too. I managed to talk with mum about her self esteem earlier that day to be clear of how she was feeling about her health, and the actions that she needed to take. Mum seemed positive about her mission in light of the fact that her own mother had been taken into hospital following a reduced eating disorder. She was distressed about the threat this situation had on her mother and (I assumed), she had thought of her own mortality. King (On looking at the present situation) agreed to wait to see what continued progress mum would make during the following week or so. I pray she would observe herself and be free to care for herself for the duration of that time for her own good.

Our time together (King and I) became very important in order to aid our transitions. This needed to be over stood on both sides. It was an extremely difficult evening and morning. I prayed for guidance as I sat with him. (How much pain can a one face in so few hours oh father, my heart feels like it will stop if I talk, help me father, my life seems to be shortening now Jah, please arm me with the ammunition I need to live and be free with your loving care right now, mighty one, please help me to talk)

I was given the time to share how my feelings were in the month of February (I had not written during that month as I felt physically, mentally, socially, intellectually, spiritually, medically and emotionally unable to cope with all that this held). I could not express the pains felt by the loss of my baby at that time because I already had more than enough children. I also knew I would have never terminated a pregnancy due to my personal ethics, I was also stuck on "I am carrying a child for a one that fills me to the brim with the energy he gives to me, it felt so good, I felt so much love in my soul for him", that I had great difficulty in accepting my loss of him as well as his baby, and the damage it had done to me. What had happened to me during February was beyond my control. I fought to hold onto myself, our baby, and to him, but it was not to be. I knew I loved the child within me with all my heart and that my love for her father would not fail to be safe in my soul, as I felt his spirit lift me so high. (Give thanks) Somehow though, I lost a part of myself that I know I will never find again. Writing right now hurts in a way that has swollen my heart and being. I need to stop for a moment.

I conceived two days after my encounter with him. I say encounter because I cannot call it anything else. We did not make love neither did we have sex. We had an encounter that broke my heart in pieces and left me to feel so completely empty. I know that only the most high could have intervened in order for me to have life again. I knew this, as I had become taken over by the spirit of the Most High, who held me passionately to aid in the conception of our spirits to form a being that will never be forgotten. I felt an overwhelming passion for King and could not control any part of it. I could not sit down; I could not stand up, I could not even think of him for fear of the presence of his face before me. This would have lead to the orgasm, which was most definitely imminent at that point in time and also to a conception. There are times when a one has no power to control, and this was that time for me, so all I could do was to fall onto my bed and beg Jah to let it all happen in the way it was to be, my orgasm took me into my golden cave to truly share the love we were placed together to share. Yes "HE", had become the Most High and we made love in a way that I could never (well maybe not now) describe to anyone, not even myself.

I cannot remember much else of what happened that day, as I was captured by my over standing of the power within me that made me happen to conceive. I know and felt that he had entered my very being, and I was consumed with a kind of love that I could not even recognise but prayed never to lose. I txt him to call him to me, I tried not to, but I needed him to know what was really happening to me. You see, I knew that I had conceived his baby, but I just couldn't find the faith within myself following our encounter, to believe it. How could I tell him that this was so for me? How could I tell him that he was whom I had prayed for and that when he touched me, I could barely breathe because of the feelings I had in my soul for him. How could I tell him that although it was not what we expected, I wanted to continue to carry his child even in spite of everything "Oh God help me to be free within this painful love that you have given to me. It hurts Jah it really hurts. Am I not to have this true love this time Jah, so that I can be free to feel what I really need this time, Jah? Free to have passion, release and conceive at a whim against all the odds and professional insight? Only you can make that be, but if it is not to be, show me Jah, just show me". I continually prayed for peace.

As I said, February was a month of transitions for me. It was also a time when my sweet child Malachi did not want to live any longer because of his own pains. Malachi and I had always been close. He had a difficult birth and had convulsions when he was only two weeks old. I kept him near me a great deal, which helped me to feel safe in the fact that he had the best care. He also had many silent needs that only I was able to fill for him as he did with some needs I had too. When we needed each other, we were just together, that's all. He had been feeling isolated in his own thoughts and could not explain them to me. He saw that I was in physical pain, especially with all the bleeding, so he felt he had nowhere to turn to for help. (No matter how you hide it, they know) He destroyed his favourite possessions, in order to be focused on, by me.

This was so painful for me that I wanted to just run or even fly away. Malachi's room had lost the Joy it had before; it just became a barren place that not even he wanted to be in, so he stayed with me in my room. I called his father who did not show his interest in my situation with his son. This also hurt me enough to leave me without hope in the safety of any my children if I had become ill in other ways, and I just did not want to go on any longer, but of course for many, thinking on life for your children without you, well it certainly aids in a swift recovery. There that's better, right as rain. I could not leave them; I had to return back to the love that I had for myself somewhere. "Show me please Jah, that you love me enough to guide me through these transitions, to make me live again, I need myself back Jah, so I can face it all. The road is too long for me to walk alone, my feet are aching".

I sought professional help for my son and it was received with thanks. It helped. I was able to express to the royal spirits in my life and my love that I needed guidance with both my feelings, and the feelings of my children. I was also deep in the middle of the organisation of a Family Cultural Event (My idea) which I felt was needed for my children and those in the community that I would always have love for, because of their support and skills that empower my family. I also knew that I had to do something major with my children so they would feel involved in something that might ease the sadness they held within them. It worked. "Blessed Jah, you are there when I call and I will follow you until you leave me, no steps to take. I will follow you until my wings can no longer be used to take off and join you".

He came to me again and I was shown that the man in my life had a strong connection with Malachi partly because of the love I held for him inside me, but also because his love for me was there as a guide. Malachi was able to see this in order that he could choose to spend quality time with a one that wanted both him and his mother in his life. The Most High showed Malachi, that King's love for him was safe and pure and that he would aid in the way forward for him. King's love was there for him because Malachi wanted it to be. My love for Malachi and for King also showed me that Malachi wanted this too.

I could not let my feelings of grief over my own loss, come in the way of the amount of repairing that was needed to be addressed in regards to Malachi or Tsion, let alone the rest of my children. There had to be a part of me that must go on to save me from more loss and grief that would come to me through the downfall of my children. I shut my feelings away and closed off my hurt, sorrow, and my need to be with the King that I loved. He too had grief to bear and my need to show him everything (I felt), would have hurt him more then he could bear at that time. It was hard, as I had to hold back on so much. In fact more than I could possibly bear at that point in time either. With the power that was within my soul and that was held within the arms of the Most High, my prayers were constantly with me. "I pray to you Jah that I may find the strength to continue to display what I feel now. Be with me oh father that I may be cleansed and be free from the bondage of this painful love that I feel within me".

QUEEN.IRENA

Black Widow

There is a deep grief within me it must be said,
That at times, I feel as a one that is bereaved.
Yes its true. When he leaves me at times,
I feel I have a broken heart left inside.
Yearning, but will have to mend soon before the morning,
So that I may handle another day's grace,
Instead of showing a gloomy face.

I feel like a black widow whose love has just died.
Empty without someone to hold me,
In the midst of the night.
Empty without a one to kiss me,
And squeeze me so wonderfully tight.
Just at times.

He leaves with a look that had said,
I have no choice but to except less.
Instead of what I deserve,
Or of what is rightfully mine, and rightfully his.
It feels so cold.
To be a part of this,
Just at times.

When we hold each other it feels so right,
Lord, for me this is a serious plight.
Would he really one day,
Be right out of my sight?
Oh Jah, that surely would be the fright of the night,
Blessed father please be prepared,

To lead me into your brightest light,

I am afraid to loose him Jah I am afraid.
Just at times.

I am the black widow that grieves but walks beside him,
Because I love him Jah, I just simply love him.
I am the black widow,
That will continue to be,
In love with him, or in love with just me.

On the inside well the pain is deep,
On the outside my royalty makes you weep.
It's just this pain Jah; it's just this pain,
That I think I will surely take to my grave.
Just at times.

Black Widow

I am a grieving Black Widow,
Who at times feels nothing but sorrow.
My love grows stronger with every day,
So reminds me when I pray,
To give thanks for what is to come,
And not just for tomorrow.

In a spin my head has been.
A broken heart between my breasts is seen.
For it is obvious there is no other way,
But to love him knowing he will never stay.
With me,
Forever and a day.   .

I am the Black Widow.
Just at times

31 LOVE IS A SPIDER'S WEB
Emails to a Queen
Opening To The Kings

My Dear Queen Imani.

I have been thinking of you this evening. I also listened to your sweet voice on a tape you gave to me of one of your radio shows. It helped me to acknowledge myself in a more positive way today. You read an extract from a book over the air. It gave me hope in the fact that there are others out there that feel as we Queens do, that shows love as we do and are an inspiration to those around them as we both are.

I also thought of a king today. I reasoned with him a little on the phone this morning. I found myself thinking on something he said and the way he said it to me. We were reasoning on the progresses of his inspirational contributions within the community, and how there had been attempts to sabotage his missions. Much as the topic of fear amongst our white counterparts regarding Black social leadership is an important one to reason on, I of course had to cut the reasoning short (The important ones seem to be very expensive, that's why my previous mobile is off). He said he would like to reason with me and he would like to see me in the week. This I agreed to do. That felt touching, and made me think of how long I had known him, and all the works we had both done, and to the heights that we had both reached. I also recognised that he is a King that had stood strong in his faith. What a blessing, Jah.

When I was asked where he lived by my king, I suddenly realised that all the years I have known him we had never reached each other's yard. That felt good too, as I became aware that at any time a one could rise and be totally inspired and move on, as the connections would always be there for the return.

I say he is a king as my reasoning with him are spiritual, emotional, educational, logical, mystical, musical and practical. He looks like a simple man, but he has the kind of wisdom and inspiration that you only pick up on (at times), long after you have finished reasoning with the I, as it is suppose to happen.

I thought of another King that I met up with on the bus today (No, yesterday now at this hour) I had noted him from since I was at school. I always saw him with his children or working within the community. We had often held hailed each other in acknowledgement, but had never talked much or even reasoned. I knew there was something about him. He is a King too. He is not aware of this yet, but it was showing brightly today and he was open to me. We reasoned on the very important things in this Livity and were both inspired. He waved vigorously to me in his purity after I got off the bus and that felt good too.

I am sure you want me to show you what else filled me today. Well, I went to collect my van and to reason with the mechanic regarding the cost (Or rather no cost). He stopped me in my tracks and showed me that he had reasoned with the other workers before I got there, (You hear me? they reasoned). They were able to show him that he could not charge me; neither must he upset me because of who I was. He told me that he valued my

152

service and that he would not hinder me with another bill to contend with. They had confessed to a previous job that they had done badly. Another blessing.

The money I was shown to give to him if he did not see the I in me, was given back to me as a test to see what I would do with it. The money went very far. In fact I know I was blessed again as I spent more than I had in the first place. I remember that I had given a bus pass that I brought away; I paid for two days meals for my cared for person, I brought some things from the bakery, something for mum and nappies for my youngest and managed to get some money swiped by the "Can I have some pocket money" crew. I started with £25.

I had a very inspiring reason with my mechanic. Yes, he is a King too believe it or not and he is certainly on a buzz. It is so good to witness it all.

I saw my sweet King. He was down and it showed, but you know what? Whether he wants to accept his royalty or not today, he most certainly and definitely IS A KING. You know that I don't have to go into any details or analysis or emphasise that fact again. It has been shown and it is seen. There is no doubt. We did not get to hold each other today, that was certainly missed by me. I wonder if he missed that too.

Having written some of the events of the day, I am aware of another situation that is happening here. I am thinking of my elder son Marcus. He needs me, (my life is like a rainbow) and I getting a message to overs his condition. He is finding life as a potential uncle and an elder brother a bit heavy. He is also feeling trapped without the ability to work and earn money. (another one of his father's doing) Omar had withdrawn his application for legal stay for Marcus because he corresponded with his birth mother. This had upset Omar to the extent that he notified his solicitor of his withdrawal as Marcus's father. With me being his only hope, I made my own application for Marcus, which was rejected. As you know, an appeal is a long process, so with any child in this situation (I pray there are not many), as being as human as they can toward trusting again, I have to work and pray hard so that my love for him could aid me in all that this work entails. Jah please bless the souls of all that are left for the vultures to pick bits off. I know the body is merely the vessel by which we are housed but at times it feels as if our souls are being physically devoured.

I know things will get easier for us all, as there are many who will aid and walk the road with the chosen. It can only bring us all to the most central part of our being which is always where only the chosen can see. If we do not acknowledge our royalty, how do we explain what we see to a one outside the royal circle? Think about it I. Why do you feel that there is something wrong with you just because what you hold within you is different. Is it because so many have no over standing of your level? This is what it is like for those who have not been chosen. No matter how you try to explain or nurse them through the heights that you have passed, the workload on you becomes too much for you, as you end up carrying them. You don't want to upset them, so you back down again. Look around, in front, behind and on both sides too. If you look inside, what a sight you see. There is no greater royalty than what you have with the true one within, because it is the true you.

Emails to a Queen
Kingdom
Poem for Kings

My dear Queen Imani.

I thought it would be a nice gesture to write regarding my thoughts on the issue of kings. I feel this because many wonder why it seems so hard for a one to identify themselves as one, while others find it difficult to think of a one that they would even give such a title. It is interesting that a one can automatically cast their minds on a Queen, while others just know they are one. I can imagine many eyes are opened wide now while they read but relax; it is not so hard to rise to this occasion. It is easier to be open to acknowledge a king, than you think.

He is a one that firstly has the utmost and warmest respect for his first love, and has no difficulty in the fact that her love for him will always be true, and be there for him too. He is able to nurse her and be attentive to her in her hours of need. He is a one that knows that his duty is at times, to take the place of his father and have the worries and the burdens that life has in store for them. He will remain strong but gentle, and give only love to his first love. He is a one that has reached ultimate heights and has floated high enough to see the glory of the almighty father with his first love and has had no fear, because of the knowledge that she would be right by his side when he needed her. She is a one that has surety in the fact that no matter what, he is her special knight in shinning armour, her prince of peace, her sweet boy, and her comfort before and after the pains of a broken heart because he is her beloved son and she is his first love, his mother.

This king? Well he is not perfect; although his aim is always for perfection, in fact he has fallen many a time to the so-called "Sins of the world" and has paid dearly. Yes he is always looking for answers to the questions within his soul. He feels like a failure often. He gets sad and frustrated, lonely, pissed off, angry, and he grieves too. He feels shame and guilt at the mistakes he has made. He challenges almost anyone; hell, he even challenges the Most High too at times. Don't worry, I have not gone mad because he is able to find peace as he also has the uprightness, willingness and ability to over stand these emotions in a way that not only aids in the repair of his soul, but also in the repair of the whole community around him. He is not afraid to express his needs wants and desires to his Queen, while aiding her to be completely expressive towards him while protecting her soul. He has the ability to bring himself back to his central being and focus on the long road ahead while remaining true to himself and his first love. We all know a one that is so. (Don't say no).

There are other issues I know that we can deal with here, but, as you know, there are many that feel we should not trouble ourselves with wondering why men find it hard to show their feelings as they are just "Dogs". Well, I beg to differ here right now. I would be so very hurt if one of my many beautiful sons were to be called a "Dog", I am no bitch. I am a mother who has nursed and held my sons. I have caressed and kissed them, I have rubbed my face and my breasts on them. I have bathed them in oils and massaged them. I have kissed every part of their hearts and their souls. I have revealed to them the Most High and have kept them safely away from harms reach. I have given up every part of my body and soul to them in order that they would come into this world and live through me. I gave them life. Please let us not collude with this westernised description of a man as a dog. We have produced princes so they may be our Kings. We have produced princesses to become our Queens.

Have you made the connection? Do you overs this reasoning? Yes, only we can produce the kings we wish to recognise; we also have the power to destroy them too. We have the true one within us as a gift from the father, so we may show them how to be and how to truly love.

When we close our eyes and meditate on our deepest love, is it not our mothers that we see? We long to be consumed with her loving touches, as we cry. Is it not the Most High that we feel and that we pray for, especially when we cannot have our mothers or our children? I mean when we are completely alone. Think of true love, real love, deep love, sensual love. Where does it come from? How do we receive it? How do we share it? When do we really need it?

The connections can only be made between us with true love as the foundation. This is not to say that those abandoned are lost forever, no way. We are all able to over stand when love is pure and true, real and right, even when our mothers are not able to love us. There will be major hurdles along the way, but the fact that we continually repair and are concerned for the safety our being is enough to get us all through with the almighty father by our side.

POEM FOR KINGS

Open your eyes and see the truth my dear King and just believe. Royalty has always been there, just for you to be aware that, no matter what you have sinned; you are still heading to be a King. Have faith and believe in the pure and true love within yourself, because this love is most certainly your royal wealth.

33.LOVE IS A SPIDER'S WEB
Emails to a Queen
Feeling Jah's Power

My dear Queen

Please forgive me if I seem low today, as you know there are times in a Queen's life (especially on particular days within our monthly transition) when a one may feel overwhelmed with a lonely grief that only the Most High can see us through. This is my time and I feel it will be especially hard for me this time. I also realise that for us Queens, this is also the time when we take our ultimate flights and reason with utmost intensity within Rastafari. May your readings be fruitful today.

I am trying to control this feeling within me but as you know my soul has been open to feel all that I desire, but this is not about my sexual feelings for him, this is about my want and need to be loved by a one that cannot allow himself to verbally express his desires to be with me, neither can he allow me to hold him in a way that will aid him in the repair of his soul (yet). This is not always a problem for me as we have an over standing of each other that include the respect for one another's space. At times through, I have been shown that he is in need of the kind of affection that only I can give him, as he only seems to aid in the repair of my emotions at particular times too. The affection that I feel also changes into a maternal one, and we women know, that this is when we become a bit more sensitive, and protective of our man's pains (Yes, they get so much pampering, till it turn's them fool) just now and then.

This is no ordinary love; this is the Royal love that I have been shown to give him. I am not saying that I do not have the same needs of him, as I most certainly do, and I have seen that too. I at times fear his rejection of this as he fights to maintain his faith in himself and the Most High order so badly that, I would rather not be around him to sense it. He cannot see what is there for him or will not. I just pray that he does not question what is to be as father can only stop that in order to move forward what we have together.

I feel that he is aware of these times for me, as I am tearful when I see him and of course the evidence is deep in my soul, which he sees in my eyes even if I try to hide it. I have been sent to him and he has been sent to me for many reasons and the natural flow of the order has shown me why. This is at times the sentence that I serve without committing the crime or merely for being who I am. I cannot caress him with my complete love because of possible rejection; he cannot do the same because of his own sentence. The only thing is that I have not rejected him and never will as the Most High has sent me to be with him. Everything that I have dreamt of him has come to pass (Erotica of us together comes to me as a gift due to my royal love desires of him) There is so much more that I have seen of him but, as you know, there are things better left for a one to discover in ones own time because of the impact it may have if more is revealed then should be. It is not good to disturb the order. Sometimes I feel angry about it all, because of the soul pains that I must experience in the process. It hurts more than I can possibly bear at times, so after a hard day, all I can do is weep until I sleep. I sleep most deeply right then and I dream the most inspiring dreams about this love, so I am compelled to write. Do not be alarmed as this is also to be. This is the order of a Queen.

During a reasoning following a most blessed night out with him, he expressed to me that he had acknowledged himself as a King.
"Almighty father when I witness your works, I see you before me. He was a glow as you are within me, and I saw it and felt it. I praise you Rastafari for choosing I n I to aid in his transition towards our royal circle. I witnessed him floating as you showed me he would. I saw his glory in every way you had shown me. Royalty flowed through that room like the liquid gold that flows through my veins. It captured me, therefore your spell was upon me so that I could leave him soon after he spoke. I thank you father".

Some time ago he talked of a true King that would soon be walking beside me. This was in relation to a one that had also recognised my Royalty. I did not comment too much at that time, as I already knew that he was talking of himself whether he was aware of it or not. It is not coincidental that he acknowledged his royal status to me following his walking with me. The fact that I had been shown him as a King beside me is something that can never be dismissed in place of another, no way, Jah. I have continued on a course that had been set for both of us no matter how strange and painful it may seem at times.

When I think of the alternative for us both, well if we are to be together at the times when we are, that is just what had been seen and will be. I certainly do not feel that I am in the way of the love he says is for him, as she most certainly is not there with him. This is not to say that I

161

have doubts when I ask him if I am in the way, I just need to confirm (as he does), that his need for the company of my soul is at the same level as it is my need for the company of his soul. And also what is to be. He is within me at all times, and physically catered for me most of the time, as I am for him. We have committed ourselves to each other's soul and have grown because of that in many ways. We have given one another continued inspiration throughout this time and have created written evidence of this love. I have certainly flown higher than I ever thought possible and have seen father often and have been taken over completely by his almighty power during our times together and times apart.

Having said what is in my heart and soul, I become increasingly aware that my need to be touched and caressed by a King who feels me within his soul, is an energy that could only have been placed inside me by the Most High. So at times I get mad with him (Father, that is). Don't get me wrong Queen, there have been the most sexual advances made towards me, especially recently. They no longer attract me though. This has happened at times even when I am definitely "On Heat". I would rather just sit and feel his energy and be consumed by his light and presence inside me when I am with King.

For the times when my body and soul longs for us to make love, well during these times, I am taken over and I am showered with the blessings of his love meeting mine within my dreams when they come to me. (What, did you think they had stopped?) No not at all. Sometimes they keep me sane as I feel I am able to release all my passions for him and that he is given the chance to release his passions with me as we swim in the midst of each other's souls. No, 'Sex' is not what I talk of here. I bring that up because we are all conditioned to think so. There is a great deal said, and attempted, in regards to the art of making love, but believe me, Queen nothing compares to the making of love with the true I within the I. I can only describe this experience as one, which can never be put into verbal reasoning, if you have never been to such heights as you just fly everlasting or float on top of a pool of water for days.

There will always be doubts in our minds and souls related to the paths that we take (I am not always free from that). These are not doubts about who we are and what we can achieve, as we all know them already. The documented evidence of our ancestors' achievements is proof enough for us all to rise. The doubts are, however usually about the reasoning behind our path choices. We have set our minds on or have wished for things and those that our eyes had seen but we cannot physically touch. We must however be careful because wishes often come true. Are we prepared for that? Or should we simply accept what our souls are crying out for (When) we recognised what is before us.

It is not just what we pray for that we receive, it is so much more. The grief and the suffering is a price we all pay for our continued search for love, as not all our foundations are as solid as we would like them to be, therefore we will always have baggage of various sizes to carry. Our own love losses tend to take its toll on our lives, so having the overs is a must now, as we might never become aware of the revelations that come to us.

Queen.

34.LOVE IS A SPIDERS WEB
Emails to a Queen

Revelations of My

SACRED EMOTIONS

Should I have held on to them and kept them buried as we are conditioned to do? No the pain would surely have consumed me. We often ask ourselves whether we should dig deeper within us to reveal our sacred emotions up onto the surface. Well, I took the plunge and delved into the very being of the I am in I, to reveal the royal love that was imprisoned within me. I was therefore faced with making the decision to accept and allow my love to grow in what ever way that kept me on the royal path, where I knew I belonged.

My sacred emotions are such that they have challenged me to the highest and deepest points of my soul. They have hurt me, accepted me, rejected and used me, taken care of me, loved me, accused me, trusted me, guided me, blessed me, reasoned with me, held me, made love to me, cried with me, laughed with me, slept with me, ignored me, fed me, starved me, grieved with me, become orgasmic with me, flown with me and released with me.

They have been and are the sweetest, most painful, happiest, most sensual and passionate emotions that have ever been bestowed on me and have inspired a deep-rooted desire within me, to remain and confirm the being of I am within the Queen that I am. This has been a sacred blessing from the Most High, which I have accepted with open arms. Unlike the others, where holding back had always been the key to remaining true to I self. There were no plans made by any mortal being in this one, the almighty father set this path for me. Yes he always alters the plans we make for ourselves, in order for us to learn. This much we all know to be true.

I have listened and reasoned with the I within I am in order to over stand the reasons why this had been such a painful transition for me. I say painful as this word is the loudest word in my soul right now, even as I type I cry. "Almighty father when I witness your works, I see you before me. He was a glow as you are within me, and I saw it and felt it. I praise you Rastafari for choosing I n I to aid in his transition towards our royal circle. I witnessed him floating as you showed me he would. I saw his glory in every way you had shown me. Royalty flowed through that room like the liquid gold that flows through my veins. It captured me therefore your spell was upon me so that I could leave him soon after he spoke. I thank you father".
Even in my dreams I tried to hold back, but the beloved King in which I adore reappeared before me and took me right back to where my sacred emotions desired to be, in his arms. You witnessed Jah, as you were there by my side and I was transformed again and again. I continued to fly during these times and I saw what you had shown to me. Why did you not leave me at that place? Why did you remove my wings and place me back on this earth, only for me to grieve again and again? What do you want from me Jah? Am I n I to end I n I days in this way?

I have released and will most likely continue, in order to dwell in the place where the I am within the I in me must be. I know I have been chosen to be so I AM, WILL BE.

The revelations within my story are as sacred as the released emotions within my soul. Did I hesitate to show them? Yes of course I did. Wouldn't you have? I advised you when you began to read about my experiences, to be true to yourself while remaining open and true to the I within me. You have had no choice but to do so, as you would have never continually consumed my writings in order to over stand the depths of this revelation.

You see Queen, I have realised something very important that had happened to me. I had been placed along a parallel path with another being (King) who is on a similar path to myself. We had been on a transition like no other. He is troubled as I am at times. Having said that, we were both placed alongside one another in order that we may protect each other's soul while we transcend. This may seem somewhat strange, but now that you have tapped into the I within yourself and the I within the I am in me so you may over stand, you have also realised the royal status you have always held within you too.

The fact still remains that I have the deepest love for this King whom I have walked with and over stood that it cannot and will not, be reproduced with another. This is a wonderful thing as he has kept the utmost respect for my soul. He has allowed me to be completely free and open about the feelings that I have for the I within him, the Most High, my mother, my Family, for my Queens, for his mother, my lovers, and of my Kings. I express how I feel whether it be of love, lust, passion, care, support or desire to him, and he has never failed from showing to me, love from his heart and from his soul because of the royal status that he has held within. He is a King that has been and is spiritually walking beside me, while protecting my soul and continually guiding thee.

The lustful dreams I have had of us together were at times a little disturbing to me because it is a part of the conditioning that had turned out to be so wrong for me, and a thing we all have to face until we troud on the paths that will help us to be free. The reality for me however, is that when I became orgasmic and I had called out his name, but not for a need for him to take the place of the Most high or of whom else I make love with when I call to him. I call, because I have only become complete with this King and no other. He was there to hold me and to protect my soul as I released my most sacred of emotions, even at times when part of his soul had been in great need of affection too. He had become open to me and shown to me, the I within the I am in him, so I happened to love him in the way I was suppose to (deeply). We took a great risk when we become intimate with our love, at a time when we were both in turmoil over the above, so we paid the price but we still managed to continually love each other. You might be asking, "What do you mean?"

I say this, because I experienced an orgasm the other night, that I did not over stand. Yes, I happened to capture it on audio. I had no memory of the occasion, only that I was in a state of semi crying mode and my mouth filled with that sweet fluid. It took a while for me to recover from this experience, as my uterus was continually contracting which made me have pain that I felt. When I played the tape back, I heard myself crying as if for help. (I had been holding back my ultimate release). I was trying to call his name but couldn't. The Most High was there and I felt myself remembering a hot presence was within me, in fact all over me at that time. While listening, I began to transcend back into the emotions that were about during the situation that was recorded. I was about to release and beginning to fly, so transcended.

{My feelings of grief had over powered me. I had held onto the deep pain of losing the baby that I had carried for the short while that it was. The baby was a symbol of perfection for me because of the royal love that I felt for him. I held onto the sexual encounter that had become so upsetting for the two of us. Being overpowered by the Most High in order to conceive, my fear, my love, my lust, my hurt, my holding back, my love again, my guilt· and my hurting of him. I think my hurting him had upset me the most because I could never take that pain back. My hurting another had always been my heaviest guilt baggage. He did not have a chance to show how he felt about a baby that he could have fathered. I had never experienced pleasurable expressions of love displayed towards me while I carried any child. I felt much pain over what I had not given him the chance to feel, and for me to experience. It had later realised that he would not have held back on the love and support that he could have offered to me.

I had been holding onto the shame and guilt of it all along with the pain of the miscarriage inside my womb. I had also held on to the guilt over hurting him there too. (Which is why I was bleeding abnormally for so long) These pains were now releasing during this orgasm. I suppose the pain had never completely left me, because I knew that this part of his pain would always be closed to me. I had put myself in isolation again and I just could not forgive myself, so it had begun to chip away at my being, like a carpenter chipping at wood. As I type, it makes me think of all the gynaecological problems that women like us have and wonder if they are due to the emotional pains that we carry around like hand bags (Which continue to be overloaded too) Yes we are super women.

My breasts continued to hurt me all the time. I was nauseous, not eating well to the extent of anaemia and had continued to feel movement within me (You know the flicker of movements a one feels while a foetus continues to develop inside its mother). The pain of the loss took me over as I even prayed that it was all a dream and I did not lose the baby at all, wishing at times that I had never had the encounter with him to begin with. Sometimes when I felt movements, I was so pleased one second and remembered the truth the next. As I type this, even the skins on my thighs have become rashes. I could scream forever over the pain that I hold. These feelings have damaged a part of the I within me, that will take forever and a day to repair, so much so that it had made my body believe that I was still pregnant. It acted as if I was too (Yes, my periods even stopped) God alone knows how so very painful this is to write about. It is even hard to believe myself that I carried these feeling without ever expressing it, but as you know by now Queen sooner or later my soul pains fly high enough to be consumed so that I rise again. Jah is always sends forth my protector.

I kept all this to myself (as I usually do) until I got a call to acknowledge what I already knew. As I began to feel that I could talk about it, there he was again, right by my side, (The King that he is) to comfort me as my guide and protector. I suppose this happened because I had read the signs from Jah through my conditioned life, and had lost faith in myself while I miscarried the precious life that was conceived between us. I lost even more while I tried to accept that he was not my Soul/King companion. I found this much too hard to face and to cope with, so I was in denial due to how deeply my feelings were for him. In fact I imagined many times, that the pain I was in would be the death of me it was so bad. This was not something that I had felt before towards anyone. Yes far out as it may seem, this was a reality that was happening to the I within the I am in me}.

I was afraid to release and reach an orgasm in case his face appeared before me while it happened. He had at times become the Most High, but he was now my spiritual guide. No, he was not making love to me, the Most High was in complete control and had demanded that. My sweet King had appeared and guided me as my soul protector. He was there, willing me to look at him and release him from this turmoil that we were both in. I did not want to orgasm, because of any sexual wants of him so I cried. His spirit held my hand and I was finally able to call his name. I felt his love, power me and I was able to release the deep-rooted pain that I had within my soul for him so that he was no longer a sexual being to me but a one that meant so much more. I was free and he was too. Oh, the pain. The Most High power had allowed him to take control and to guide me through a very painful and intense orgasm that I had never experienced before and never will forget. He flew with me, and oh my, what a truly blessed flight it was. (Absolutely Sacred) It took me a while to recover from this and still makes me cry when I think of what happened to me with the experience of that orgasm, but also over all the love and the pain and the sweetness that I had experienced over the past eight months.

There became a corner of my soul that had been touched by a precious angel sent by the Most High to watch over me. Most of us do not usually realise this happening, because of our conditioning. We fall in love and try to follow the others and all hell breaks loose. You hurt me, and I hurt you. You never said, and should have, and I never knew, and was not listening. We are supposed to see, with every part of our being, and accept the lessons we learn from the emotions felt. This is not an easy task.

The pain experienced in the process of not seeing and listening is extreme and can damage every part of our soul. We become the flies stuck in the spider's web struggling to prevent ourselves from being devoured by the almighty spider. Our hearts, minds and souls are in danger if we do not have faith in the I within us, see the truth and believe. I know that my true love is within the I am in me. I also know that a precious, royal and powerful guide has both guided and protected my soul during this transition towards the deepest love of all.

I give the most thanks to the Most High for his selection and I give thanks for the quality of love that has reached out from the I within this King and has guided the I within this Queen. We are both here for the same reasons. We have both been placed here on a mission. It is all about love, only not as we are taught to over stand it. This is not an everyday love thing; we have all had that, and know every corner of the ups and downs that comes with it. I know that the I am within me had been given a love that had made me fly so high that I call Jah

Rastafari in praise. I also know that King is blessed each time I hear his name in my travels.

The sacred emotions that have been captured within my soul by the love I feel for him, are a gift from the Most High. He, powered by the Most High, is the only one that can explain the love that he feels for me and shows to me within his own words of songs. This is a reward for the love that I give to him and all that are in my life and my love. It feels wonderful, although at times so extremely painful, but it is also protected by the Most Highest power that I know is true. There is no doubt in my being, that he is most certainly nothing but a King, whose memory of sweet love and strength will remain within me while I n I heart beats and is deep-rooted within I n I soul.

I n I will never again write in this way of I n I feelings for I n I true Spiritual King, I n I Sweet Love. Sealed by Selah.
Queen.Irena

35. LOVE IS A SPIDER'S WEB

Emails to a Queen
'I AM' is 'THE ONE'

Dear Queen Imani

Thinking and thinking leaves a one in a spin,
Into many different circles,
For years without a break,
For just plain living.

But when it is no longer bearable,
And we are about to give up and give in,
The end of it all comes (The release)
So what on earth is keeping us going?

The Will is a being that has many legs,
If we lose one, well we have others,
And somehow we manage.
To limp along until,
Another leg becomes damaged.
Jah, we are about to die,
When another part,
Of our body is devoured.

How the hell are we?
To cope with the blow
Of a lost mother, father,
Or a lost child's soul
That is hard enough to oversee,
But how do we deal,
With the loss,
Of the will to be.

We make many sacrifices,
To remain with the true one within,
In order for us to have faith in the rewards,
Of our hopes and of our dreams.

Is it faith that keeps us together?
Or is it the will to,
Over power the pain of it all.
No I do not have the answers unfortunately,
I just go on and on like,
An everlasting bouncing ball.

35.LOVEIS A SPIDERS WEB
Emails to a Queen

No time to ponder and nowhere to wonder,
Got too many lives,
To keep in order.
No time to work,
No time to play,
Too far to walk to catch my water.

Too many minds to straighten,
Hearts to mend that have been broken.

Too many souls to join with,
That will make us feel good.
Too many trees to chop down,
In order to collect their wood.

Too many shoes to buy in the sales,
Pretty letters that turn out to be bills.
Too many meetings to meet,
Oh I just remembered,
I've had nothing to eat.

My oh my,
The pools in my eyes,
It's no wonder,
That there had to be a "Sacrifice"

In order to make the sacrifices that we do,
We have to give in to the most burning of issues.
In our lives at that present moment,
It could be anything,
But it usually is something.

That is unpleasant,
But needs to be done,
What other reason,
Would there be for a one,

To do a thing that is unpleasant or upsetting,
It is usually something,
That we will never be forgetting.
That makes us feel hurt,
Disrespected, victimised and alone.
Angry, sad, taken advantaged of,
Or just plain trodden upon.

35.LOVEIS A SPIDERS WEB
Emails to a Queen

Why on earth would a one have,
To accept such a plight.
Is it because of the will to live,
Or is it knowing,
That the end is in sight?

The end of what?
The pain, the suffering,
Or the end of life itself,
Who can answer that?
Do you believe you can?
Or have you just
Merely forgotten you wealth.

You do have the answers,
As we all do.
We know why we take the paths,
We have trodden on,
Because we have made the choices,
Yes I have and you have too.

Whether for good or for bad.
We know why,
We end up in those situations,
When we recognise,
That we have been had.

No, I am not saying,
That we plan our pains,
All I say is that,

We become aware,
Of what we have gained.

From knowing how,
It all happened, after the event,
Now that's not so hard,
Not if you know to where you had been sent.

("If only I knew……….")
Was born to even virgins when caught,
As it has become
A well-used catch phase,
As we knew those words would.

.

35.LOVEIS A SPIDERS WEB
Emails to a Queen

We could punch the walls,
For the mad, wild and stupid ness of it all,
When we learn,
That our backs are truly against the wall,
Then we get logical and make,
More choices in order to
Prevent other mistakes.

Well you know that's where the sacrifices come in,
And when we begin to suffer,
Because for us to return back home,
To The One within ourselves,
We have to pray deep within,
And not outside to another.

For life itself dwells right there,
Because you become suddenly aware,
That the only way forward,
Is to sacrifice yourself or disappear.

So you begin to have faith,
That your Will to live is real,
It just keeps you holding on,
Or otherwise you most certainly become ill.

So you now see a light,
At the end of the tunnel,
Yes there may at times,
Be a small candle flickering, (Instead)

Of a strong light,
That you know is,
Just about to go dead.

But the faith that the small candle will
Continue to burn a little longer,
Is like watching a vehicle's petrol gauge,
That has long past the red.

35.LOVE IS A SPIDERS WEB

Emails to a Queen

There is a mission,
Within our souls,
That we know has to be,
An axe to grind,
At the end of the pain,
In order to be free.

A book to read, that tells the world,
Of what a Queen,
Had been through,
Thousands of songs to sing (by a King)
To aid millions,
Over stand the effects,
On the I within me,
And the I within you.

Hell to pay,
If a one attempts,
To judge or bump you,
Bad words to cuss,
For those who may,
Treat us like fools.

As for the Most High 'I'
Well don't cry,
as he will continually relieve us,
From feeling, that we would sink.

So to Rastafari my highest bewilder, I give thanks,
I have two legs left, if nothing else,
And two golden wings,

181

So I may fly and return back home,
To The "I Am" within I n I self.

Love will eternally be spinning A Spider's Web.

'Closing Prayer'

WE PRAY

Merciful father, hear our prayer,
For our Souls that are troubled.
Hold us, in your mystical arms,
And carry us when we stumble.

Walk with us, both day and night,
And we will begin to notice your face.
So you will forever be in our sights,
To save us from any disgrace.

Wash me in liquid gold, oh Jah,
Cleanse my soul too,
And reveal to them,
What you have revealed to me
As that power, I do not hold.

We look to the I AM in you,
To guide us through, this time,
I know, we have asked of you so much,
We are your royal party, that you placed on this earth,
We, are back together again,
Your Kingdom, has that magic touch.   .

But you already know that,
So hear our plea to you, Father,
This is not a waste of time, for a start,
We have carried the very best of you,
Placed within our core, and written on our hearts.

Within us, these emotions had always been,
Following your continual signs,

Only, the roads are at times, so hard to walk upon,
Although, we aim never decline.

But the power of your love, Oh Jah!
The power of your love,
We truly know you have been there,
Besides us and in our hearts,
We felt you there since the beginning,
Yes, besides us from the very start.

Selah.

Queen.Irena

Love is a Spider's Web
(Emails to a Queen)

Extra

NO REGRETS

FOR THE

PLEASURES

NO REGRETS

FOR THE
PLEASURES
THAT I N I KEEP

185

MY ULTIMATE SEXUALITY

I awoke in the usual state I find myself in at these times (Completely Horny), so I sent another txt. This time to a one that had not only tasted me, but also wanted and needed more of me, and I certainly had craved for more of him for a while. He was ready and able right then, so he txt me to call him. He sounded so sexy that I wanted him instantly, but we both had to wait until later that day when I could get to him.

I had barely got in the door and he was reminding me of the mission at hand. I wanted a drink of course, and possibly something to eat. I needed food (You know the coo, no time to eat before I reached him). I got a drink. We lay on the bed and started to chat and, well forget that. We stood up and I had to get his clothes off him and he had to suck my breasts. As we panted and stumbled, I noticed his very large hood. I couldn't believe that I hadn't noticed it before. I laughed in shock and asked how he would fit it inside me. Well all he could say was "Just wait, you will feel how". I couldn't wait. We fell back onto the bed and frantically kissed and sucked each other while putting on his protection. He entered me abruptly and I certainly felt it. He was so large and stiff that I didn't know how I would cope with the sweetness of it. My god, I felt full. I had to instantly plunge my teeth into his shoulder, instead of screaming so soon. He held onto my head and frantically kissed my lips, neck and breasts. I held his head and done the same with him. We weren't even heated up yet.

He stopped! "What! You better not stop," I said. He looked at me and laughed and said, "Why, what do you want me to do with you then my Queen?" I pushed his head back and said, "I want you to fuck me all over". He began again even harder. Oh Jah, the sweet pain plunged through me like a train going through a tunnel (Don't pretend you didn't just get a flash of yourself getting a fuck on that train just then, because I don't believe you) "Is this what you want my Queen? I am your faithful servant my Queen. You said, you were hungry, for a fuck, and a screw, because you, were feeling, so horny". He pushed with every second or third word. (Each time he thrust himself into me, I bit my bottom lip, tossed my head to and thro and fucked him right back crying out over the sweet deep painful feelings inside me. It made the whole of my being, water) "My Queen, does this taste good? Your servant is here Queen, I am here to fuck, and screw, and suck, and to lick you my Queen." He whispered into my ear. "Your pussy, is so hot and sweet, I want it, and I love it, oh, my Queen." I just melted with his words, while I kissed him and groaned in pleasure. Licking and kissing lips in passion, I flooded him with my juices shouting, " Ah yes, just don't stop, I've wanted this for too long Oh Oh." He stopped and said "You want me to stop then Queen?" I couldn't believe he done that. "No, no fuck me" I demanded, holding onto his buttocks so he couldn't get away "Is that yes fuck, or no fuck" he asked. "Oh my god, (I could just eat him or kill him right now) Yes, Fuck Me, Fuck Me," I screamed while dancing with him for dear life. We were so hot and slippery; that we slipped our bodies all over each other. His strong firm figure was devouring my deep succulent body, and I absolutely loved it. I bit, scratched, pinched and licked him while we fucked and fucked. He groaned with delight, and I screamed with this sweetest of passions as I reached my juiciest of orgasms. "Sweets" I uttered that Sweet King's name. (Thank god this lover did not hear me). It just came out. A slight spill out of the soul (Yes, he was there within me, as he had been for a while) I did not hold back on any noise, moves, or words. We were both experienced enough to know about the importance of releasing all of the passion felt at these times.

We knew that we could not stop right away, so we took it slowly and gently now. The panting was strong, but we had become calmer and more controlled. I could not believe what he had just done to me but I should not have been surprised, as I had seen him as a possible grand lay even Ten years ago, when many wanted to experience a piece of him. I did wonder why at times. I suppose I always knew there was a possibility that we would connect sooner or later. When we met in the street and talked, there was always a sexual chemistry that was never ventured between us. Right now that was not important, as what was happening within our present encounter was so tasty. He smelt sweet, and good enough to eat (You know the kind of man I mean, sexy) I felt myself rising back to him, while I thought of him years ago. He had not stopped licking and kissing me, so he was ready. We turned onto our sides and fucked again. We were so wet; there was a large wet patch in the place where we had laid earlier. I didn't know my legs could reach so high. "Oh no, no, oh no" I could feel myself coming again.

This was not like me, not so often and with a man. I thought. "Yes, come on Queen," he said "You can do it, come on, let go on me, drown me with more of your sweet, hot juices. Come all over me and wet me up while you suck me inside your juicy pussy." (I feel like I am about to come as I write this, but I won't) I can just see, feel and taste him right now. I want to just lick him all over again. Oh, my pussy. I was really trying not to come again with him. (I suppose another condition that all women are under. Don't let them feel that you belong to them). What a load of rubbish. I loved it too much to hold back on a single thing. He was sensually bountiful to me and I just wanted every donation he was offering. Right then, I belonged to him alone and he most certainly was absolutely all mine. " Oh, My, God, What are you doing to me?" I cried out. "What you asked for, My Sweet, Juicy, Sexy Queen". He replied. We were so engulfed with the desire for passion that we fought wildly together in search for more. I felt completely ravenous, so melted with the heat. I was on fire, burning hot fire.

The heat made me fly up so high it overtook me. I had no idea what happened to me right then, but I knew I couldn't stop until it was over for me, and for him. I witnessed him tear his protection off and pour himself onto me while in his sweet pain. He cried out and I held him and gasped for breath as I was on the tip of another orgasm in disbelief. He noticed but collapsed, he had reached his peak. "I know you were about to fly again," he said, "But I just could not hold onto it". I was unable to talk just then but indicated to him that it was all right. My heart was pounding and about to explode. I felt for my pussy and it had flooded but was throbbing. For a few seconds, I thought (What a wonderful way to die). Still panting, I turned and said accusingly, "You are serious trouble" "I know" he replied through his laugh. We lay there a while to catch our breath. Recovered, I got up, showered and left him in no condition to leave for work. I was not in much of a condition myself, but had to walk down the stairs and even drive. I don't know how I managed to do it.

I staggered into my vehicle and paused to remember where I was, and who I was. I drove like a man. I took the wrong turning a few times in my confusion, as all I could do was laugh out loud and grin about the events with him. I screamed with the naughtiness and excitement of it all. It was so passionate and juicy and sexy and tasty and pussy and cocky. What a Fuck. I had to hold onto the steering wheel in the traffic jam and bow my head as I thought, because you know what? I had another orgasm on the way home. Boy, I am so horny. (Remember the song that you might have objected to before?) Well, if you, ever experienced what I just describe, then you could see where that sister was coming from.

When I got home, I managed to cook a little but had to retire to my bed. I just could not cope with keeping upright. The ground was pulling me down. My neck, back bottom, thighs, arms, shoulders and most of all my pussy were in pain. I did not dare go to the toilet yet, as I know I would cry with the burning pain that I would have to face. I was right. It burned like hot pepper sauce. It took almost a week for my body to cope with the physical effects of that day, but it was more than worth it. As for my mind, well every time I think of it, I have to laugh and hold myself. I reflect on it every day and have to bite my bottom lip, close my eyes, smile and shake my head. I am sure YOU MUST know the reasons why.

Queen.Irena

GLOSSARY

In order to keep up with the pace of my life, I would like to introduce a short summary of my thoughts on the decision that I have made regarding an exclusion of a Glossary describing the characters, (Particularly of my children) in my story.

I do not feel that to include a glossary, would help to maintain the continuity of emotional, and spiritual privacy that is found in the foundation of my family. I have worked hard, and have made every effort to be true to their feelings, and have followed both verbal and none verbal family ethics; not allowing details regarding their personal issues, becoming completely apparent.

This book contain details of my adult life, which I conduct separate to the life that I maintain with my children. In order to do this, I lightly loosened the tap and express, a small percentage of my emotions, in relation to how I feel about their plights, and the reasons why their lives are tough.

I have focused my writings, on my personal feelings, and responses to them baring in mind that my readers may identify with them occasionally. Having said this, its focus will by no way paint a complete picture of myself, but would merely sketch out, just eight months worth, of responses to life long lessons.

The names of the characters that visit my life in those months, be it intimate or otherwise have been changed in order to protect their confidentiality. Only the names of myself, my Queen Imani and that of my mother Queen Dowlyn remain unchanged.

I therefore give the chosen names of my children in order of age and how they relate to me.

Name	Relationship
Tsion	Daughter (Princess)
Marcus	Son (Prince)
Ezekiel	Son (Prince)
Malachi	Son (Prince)
Erran	Son (Prince)
Arran	Son (Prince)
Nathan	Son (Prince)

Fig. 1 Table of Children

A Can of Madness

By Jason Pegler

Britain's answer to Prozac Nation is the book that inspired the setting up of Chipmunkapublishing. This autobiography on manic depression takes you to the edge of the abyss and then helps you to recover.

Order online or write a cheque made payable to Chipmunkapublishing for £12 and send it to Chipmunkapublishing, PO Box 6872, Brentwood, Essex, CM13 1ZT.

ISBN 09542218 2 6

WWW.CHIPMUNKAPUBLISHING.COM

World Is Full Of Laughter

By Dolly Sen

The acclaimed autobiography on manic depression and child abuse.

Order online or write a cheque made payable to Chipmunkapublishing for £12 and send it to Chipmunkapublishing, PO Box 6872, Brentwood, Essex, CM13 1ZT.

ISBN 0 9542218 1 8

WWW.CHIPMUNKAPUBLISHING.COM

The Naked Bird Watcher

By Suzy Johnston

The highly acclaimed and positive autobiography on manic depression from a talented lady in Scotland.

Order online or write a cheque made payable to Chipmunkapublishing for £12 and send it to Chipmunkapublishing, PO Box 6872, Brentwood, Essex, CM13 1ZT.

ISBN 0 9542218 3 4

WWW.CHIPMUNKAPUBLISHING.COM

Who Cares?

By Jean Taylor

An autobiography on manic depression from a survivor and carer from Blackpool.

Order online or write a cheque made payable to Chipmunkapublishing for £12 and send it to Chipmunkapublishing, PO Box 6872, Brentwood, Essex, CM13 1ZT.

ISBN 0 9542218 5 0

WWW.CHIPMUNKAPUBLISHING.COM

The Necessity of Madness

By John Breeding

A counselor and activist tells us in a simple way how madness is a metaphor and psychiatry is a clinical construct.

Order online or write a cheque made payable to Chipmunkapublishing for **£30** and send it to Chipmunkapublishing, PO Box 6872, Brentwood, Essex, CM13 1ZT.

ISBN 0 9542218 77

WWW.CHIPMUNKAPUBLISHING.COM

Poems of Survival

By Sue Holt

Powerful poetry of a manic depressive battling for survival. Extremely moving and honest.

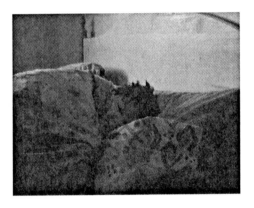

Order online or write a cheque made payable to Chipmunkapublishing for £12 and send it to Chipmunkapublishing. PO Box 6872, Brentwood, Essex, CM13 1ZT.

ISBN 09542218 9 3

WWW.CHIPMUNKAPUBLISHING.COM

Don't Look Back In Anger

By Phillip Pettican

An autobiography on Schizophrenia with an amazing transformation half way through the book.

Order online or write a cheque made payable to Chipmunkapublishing for £12 and send it to Chipmunkapublishing, PO Box 6872, Brentwood, Essex, CM13 1ZT.

ISBN 09542218 6 9

WWW.CHIPMUNKAPUBLISHING.COM

Love Is A Spider's Web

By Queen Irena

This sensuous mother of seven and care has a real story of survival to tell.

Order online or write a cheque made payable to Chipmunkapublishing for £12 and send it to Chipmunkapublishing, PO Box 6872, Brentwood, Essex, CM13 1ZT.

ISBN 19046970 0 3

WWW.CHIPMUNKAPUBLISHING.COM

Why Me?

Tony Hurley

Experiences of manic depression from an open university graduate.

Order online or write a cheque made payable to Chipmunkapublishing for £12 and send it to Chipmunkapublishing, PO Box 6872, Brentwood, Essex, CM13 1ZT.

ISBN 190469702 X

WWW.CHIPMUNKAPUBLISHING.COM

A Can of Madness Play

Adapted for stage by Robert Hutchinson and Jason Pegler

Sit and understand manic depression for the very first time, you can see how manic depression feels from the inside

ISBN 1 9046970 1 1

WWW.CHIPMUNKAPUBLISHING.COM

First showing February 2003

Chipmunkapublishing

PROMOTING POSITIVE IMAGES OF MENTAL DISTRESS

THE MENTAL HEALTH SURVIVOR'S PUBLISHER

WWW.CHIPMUNKAPUBLISHING.COM

Printed in the United Kingdom
by Lightning Source UK Ltd.
9806300001B/55-84